There's something mysterious, exciting and a little sinister, too, about the house Bosie, Clara and Noel have come to stay in. Surrounded by its overgrown garden, no other houses in sight, it looks lonely. And are the shuttered windows to keep burglars out, or to keep people in – like a prison?

Everything seems strange to the three children, staying in the country with grandparents they've never met till now, while their father recovers from his illness. There's a lot to explore, and they make some odd discoveries, like the nest of mice in an old sofa – and the gun stored away in an attic. They uncover secrets about people, too – why their mother and her parents quarrelled, why their grand-mother lets Mrs Battle the housekeeper tyrannize her and, most unsettling of all, that there's somebody who thinks he has at least as much right in the house as they have. When David inserts himself into the household, Clara, Bosie and Noel don't know what to make of him. Friendly and pleasant on the surface, is he really a sinister threat to their vulnerable group of the very old and the very young? Or is he something else altogether?

Kept in the Dark has all the suspense of a detective story, but the mystery is really one of why people behave the way they do. And the author shares her fascination so skilfully that you won't want to stop reading till you've unravelled the last clue.

Other books by Nina Bawden

CARRIE'S WAR
THE FINDING
A HANDFUL OF THIEVES
ON THE RUN
THE PEPPERMINT PIG
REBEL ON A ROCK
THE ROBBERS
THE RUNAWAY SUMMER
THE SECRET PASSAGE
SQUIB
THE WHITE HORSE GANG
THE WITCH'S DAUGHTER

NINA BAWDEN

Kept in the Dark

PUFFIN BOOKS

Puffin Books, Penguin Books Ltd, Harmondsworth, Middlesex, England
Viking Penguin Inc., 40 West 23rd Street, New York, New York 10010, U.S.A.
Penguin Books Australia Ltd, Ringwood, Victoria, Australia
Penguin Books Canada Limited, 2801 John Street, Markham, Ontario, Canada L3R 1B4
Penguin Books (N.Z.) Ltd, 182–190 Wairau Road, Auckland 10, New Zealand

First published by Victor Gollancz Ltd 1982
Published in Puffin Books 1984
Reprinted 1985, 1987

Filmset in 10/12 Linotronic Plantin by
Rowland Phototypesetting Ltd
Bury St Edmunds, Suffolk
Printed and bound in Great Britain by
Cox & Wyman Ltd, Reading

For Jessica Bawden

CHAPTER

1

'David's coming next weekend,' Grandpa said.

He spoke in a threatening voice – as if David was a savage tiger coming to visit them. But that was only his manner. He said things like 'Pass the salt' in much the same tone. And the children, Noel and Clara and Bosie, sitting at the breakfast table and trying to eat lukewarm, lumpy porridge, were too busy thinking about what was happening to them just at that moment to pay much attention to what might be going to happen. Too busy listening to the sounds their mother was making upstairs. The to-and-fro of her feet on the polished boards of the bedroom above as she took her clothes out of the closet. Packing her suitcase. Preparing to leave them . . .

'David's coming, didn't you hear me?' Grandpa crackled the thin, single page of the letter and glared at their grandmother over his spectacles. Clara and Bosie hunched their shoulders, heads bent over their plates of horrible porridge. This was nothing to do with them – they didn't know who David was, after all. Only Noel, the oldest, saw his grandmother draw a sharp breath and blink. She had naked looking, shiny eyes, and her wrinkled lids came down like shutters.

'Like a lizard blinking,' Noel thought, and wanted to laugh suddenly, because 'Liz' was what she had asked the children to call her. Elizabeth was her name, of course, but Liz was short for lizard, too. And she had a habit of staying very still, motionless except for blinking occasionally, and then scuttling quickly off, through a door, out of sight. A habit, perhaps, that years of living with Grandpa had taught her? Keep quiet. Lie low. *Hide*.

Was she scared of Grandpa? Noel guessed that she might be, but it was only a guess. This was the first time Noel and Clara and Bosie had met their grandparents, the first time they had ever been in their house, and there was no reason, Noel told himself, to be afraid of a person just because he had a big, mottled, red and blue face, a loud voice, and hard, heavy, cold hands. Last night, when they came, as they stood in the hall, he had looked at them for some time in silence, then touched each of their heads in turn with his stiff, chilly fingers, before saying slowly, on a long drawn out breath, 'Ah! Here we are, then! The little children of the poor.'

Noel had seen his mother frown, but she had said nothing. As Liz, his grandmother, said nothing now.

Grandpa growled at her, 'You've no objection, I take it? Liberty Hall. Let them all come! Isn't that how you like it?'

Liz still didn't answer. She blinked, her lizard's sudden blink, and put her hand down to touch the old dog, a black labrador that sat at her feet, leaning against her, grey muzzle propped on her knee.

Grandpa said, 'David's had a rough time, it seems. Things haven't been easy.'

'Not for anyone, lately. Have they, old fellow?' Though Grandma-Liz appeared to be addressing this remark to the dog, fondling his ears and gazing into his mild, milky eyes, there was a note in her voice as if she were warning Grandpa to be kind, to be careful.

'Ah!' he said. 'Hmph! All right. Point taken.'

After that, no one spoke for a minute. The dining-room door stood wide open and the listening children heard the two sharp clicks as their mother fastened her suitcase. Noel and Clara looked at each other. Bosie slid off his chair.

Grandpa thumped the table, making the cups dance. 'Ambrose! Sit down! Finish your breakfast!'

'I have finished,' Bosie said. 'All I want. I know porridge is good for you, but I don't really like it.'

And he was out of the room before Grandpa could speak again, thudding up the stairs.

Liz said, 'Perhaps you should go, Noel. Your mother's case will be heavy for Bosie.'

'*Ambrose!*' Grandpa said. 'For better or worse, and not my choice, I can tell you, but the child's name appears to be Ambrose.'

Clara said, 'But Bosie is what he's used to. He's always called Bosie at home.'

'In Rome you do what the Romans do,' Grandpa said. He laughed, showing a fine set of long, strong, yellow teeth. He grinned with these teeth, sharp as old fangs, at Noel and Clara. 'And in this bit of Rome, I'm the Chief Roman.'

Since they saw he meant to make a joke, they smiled

9

dutifully. Noel said, 'May I leave the table, Grandpa? To help with the suitcase.'

'Apparently you may. It seems that your grandmother has given you her permission. I may be master of the house, but she is mistress at her own table.'

'Yes, sir,' Noel said. 'Thank you, sir.'

But Bosie was already down the stairs, lugging the case, the weight tugging him sideways. He was willing, but he was only ten, and small for his age. His face was pink with effort and his eyes were starting tears. When Noel took the case from him, he turned to his mother and hid his face in her side. She had her old coat on, the ancient fox collar turned up, and her face looked narrow and pale in its frame of golden fur. She said, 'Hush, Bosie darling, it's all right, it's *going* to be all right, please don't cry. I'll be back very soon. And you'll have a splendid time! This nice, big house in the country! You've never lived in the country before. You'll see what fun it can be, all the lovely woods and the fields . . .'

Stroking the back of his head, pressing the nape of his neck with her fingers, she looked at Noel and Clara and managed a small, encouraging smile to try and comfort them, too. But when she spoke they had the feeling that she wasn't really talking to them, but to Grandpa and Liz. She said, 'I was always so happy here.'

'Well, that's something,' Grandpa said. 'That's an admission. I suppose we ought to be grateful, even if it's taken you a long time to make it. Still, bygones be bygones, and I won't hold it against you. Nor bar the door. Our house has always been open to you, even though you chose not to enter it. Now that you've changed your mind, if only to suit yourself, you're welcome to stay. What's to stop you? David's coming, but there's plenty of room; he can sleep in the attic.'

'Who's David?' she asked, without interest. She shook her head and sighed.

Clara said, 'She has to be with Dad, Grandpa. He'd be lonely without her. It'll be bad enough for him, being lonely for us.'

'A man should be a man, in my opinion,' Grandpa said. 'Support his wife and his children. If he can't do that, then he shouldn't whine.'

Clara turned red. She opened her mouth, then closed it again. Dumb with rage.

Her mother said quickly, 'He's done his best. Now he's ill and I have to look after him, and you have to look after Noel and Clara and Bosie. I know it's a nuisance, a fearful intrusion into your comfortable life, and if I had any alternative I would have taken it. But there's no one else I could turn to. I'm sorry.'

She didn't sound sorry. She was as angry as Clara.

'That's enough!' Grandpa shouted, getting up from the table and advancing towards her. 'Do what you want to do, make your bed, lie on it. But please don't insult me. I know my duty, I hope, and I'll do it.'

'Duty?' she said. 'That's a cold word to use about your own grandchildren.'

'What else do you expect?'

'Love,' she said. 'Kindness.' And, to the children's amazement (she sounded so furious they had thought she might fly at him, hit him as she hit their father sometimes when she lost her temper) she stretched up her hands to draw his face down to hers and kissed his rough, purple cheek. She said softly, 'Be kind to them. Whatever has happened, whatever I've done, it isn't their fault.'

'Hmph!' he said. 'Well.' He touched the place where her lips had been, as if to hold the kiss there. Then said –

mumbled, rather – 'Anything you need. Any help. You've only to ask.'

'Oh, no,' she said, brisk again, backing away from him, smiling brightly. 'You're doing quite enough, thank you!'

	Mon	Tues	Wed	Thurs	Fri	Sat
Richmond 940 0981/6857						
Term Time Only	2-6	2-5	2-6	2-6	2-6	10-5
}	10-1	10-1	10-1	10-1	10-1	10-5
School Holidays }	2-6	2-5	2-6	2-6	2-6	
Twickenham 892 8091 }	10-1	10-1	10-1	Closed	10-1	10-5
}	2-6	2-8	2-5		2-6	
East Sheen 876 8801	10-6	10-8	10-5	Closed	10-6	10-5
Teddington 977 1284	10-6	10-5	10-8	Closed	10-6	10-5

Ham	940 8703)						
Hampton	979 5110)						
Whitton	894 9828)	10-6	10-8	10-5	Closed	10-6	10-5
Kew	876 8654)						

THE ABOVE 4 LIBRARIES CLOSED FOR LUNCH DAILY: 12.30-1.30

| Castelnau | 748 3837) | 10-6 | 10-5 | 10-8 | Closed | 10-6 | 10-5 |
| H.Hill | 979 3705) | | | | | | |

CLOSED FOR LUNCH DAILY: 12.30-1.30

| Heathfield | 894 1017 | 10-6 | 10-5 | 10-8 | Closed | 10-6 | 10-5 |

CLOSED FOR LUNCH DAILY: 1.00-2.00

| H. Wick | 977 1559 | 3-6 | 3-5 | 3-8 | Closed | 3-6 | 10-5 |

CLOSED FOR LUNCH SATURDAY: 12.30-1.30

CHAPTER
2

The children went with her, out to the car. It looked small and dirty on the white gravel drive. Like a battered toy someone had abandoned.

Bosie said, 'Grandpa has a Bentley. I saw it last night when I put my bike in the garage. Do you think he'll take us out in it?'

'If he still drives. He's very old, Bosie.' She opened the car door, took the suitcase from Noel, and threw it on the back seat. Then looked at the three of them, standing round her. 'They're both old,' she said. 'Don't forget that. About as old as the century. Grandpa is over eighty. Your grandmother a year or two younger. Maybe three years. I've forgotten, exactly.'

'She asked us to call her Liz,' Bosie said. 'I thought that was funny.'

'Maybe she doesn't feel like being a grandmother. She hasn't had much practice at being one, has she? I expect she feels a bit shy with you.'

Noel wanted to cry. He could feel the tears swelling up. To stop them he said, with a silly laugh, 'Liz. Short for *lizard*. That's what I thought of. So skinny and wrinkled and quick.'

'That's not very kind, is it, Noel?'

Clara rushed to defend him. 'It's not *unkind*, either. Just what he thinks she looks like. He hasn't said it to her. So don't be mean, Mum.'

'Sorry,' she said, at once. Apologizing – but to Clara, not Noel. He saw this resentfully. Then she said, smiling at him, 'She used to be very pretty. When I was your age, I thought she was beautiful.'

She hugged them in turn. An extra tight squeeze for Bosie, the baby. She got into the car, closed the door with a slam, switched on the engine, wound down the window. 'Now. No point in hanging about. You'll get cold and I've got a long drive to London. Any last questions?'

Though she sounded cheerful, it seemed to Noel that she was watching them sadly. *He* would be sad, he thought, saying goodbye to *his* children.

Bosie said, 'How long do we have to stay?'

'You know that, Bosie dear. I've already told you. Until Dad is better. Until he's out of the hospital and one of us has a job.'

'We could have stayed at home,' Clara said. 'You could have gone to London to be near Dad in the hospital, and we'd have looked after ourselves.'

'It wasn't suitable,' her mother said. 'Even if we could have afforded to keep the house on, children have to be properly cared for. You're lucky to have grandparents willing to do it.' She regarded them half sternly, half

14

teasing. 'So please behave well. They don't *have* to like you, so you had better try and be nice and agreeable. Stop pulling faces Bosie – this includes *you*! Don't pull faces at Grandpa, or behind his back, either. And keep your fingers out of other people's purses and pockets.'

'I stopped stealing last year,' Bosie said. 'On my birthday.'

'Well, don't start again. For my sake. Your grandfather would blame me and Dad, say we should have brought you up better. And Clara –' She looked at Clara, eyes dancing. 'Clara, my darling, don't swear. And try not to rant and rage every time you think something's wrong or unfair. You can't put the world to rights by yelling and screaming.'

Clara tossed her long hair back, proud of the part her mother had given her. Clara the Wild One, the passionate person.

Noel said eagerly, 'What about me? What mustn't I do?'

'Oh, Noel, I don't know . . .' She thought for a moment, then laughed. 'Just don't be *too* good and show up the others!'

Noel shrivelled with shame. Was that all she could think of? To be good wasn't interesting. *He* wasn't interesting was what she was saying – not like Bosie and Clara. The Little Thief, the Proud Girl with the Terrible Temper. But he wasn't going to let her see he was hurt. Eyes burning, he said, 'I'll do my best, but I can't really tell how I'm going to be. It's so odd. Staying with strangers who ought not to be strangers. Grandparents. I mean, I know that you and Dad quarrelled with them, but we didn't, did we? Why didn't we ever see them? Didn't they want to see us?'

'Yes,' his mother said. 'Yes, they did.' She was quiet,

15

frowning a little, staring through the windscreen. 'That was my fault. But I thought I was right. They didn't like Dad, didn't want me to marry him, and when I did, Grandpa refused to see him. So I wouldn't come here alone, or let you come, either. Please try to understand, darlings. If they didn't want us all, as a family, then I made up my mind they wouldn't have anyone. And I wouldn't give in.'

'Well, you've had to now, haven't you?' Clara said. She laughed as if this was funny, but Noel knew from the way her eyes had turned from bright, piercing blue to a dark, smoky colour, that she was beginning to boil up inside.

'You shouldn't have said that,' Noel told her, when the rusty old car had shot off down the drive, back-firing and spluttering. 'I think she was crying.'

'Serve her right,' Clara said. 'Leaving us!' Her eyes were still stormy. She kicked at the gravel. 'Grown-ups are horrible. Always expecting you to understand how they feel. "Please try to understand, darlings!" Bloody hell, why should we bother? It's nothing to do with us, is it? Mum and Dad quarrelling with Grandpa and keeping it up all these years. And not really explaining! That's something else horrible about grown-ups. They only ever tell you half of a thing. The interesting bits are always kept secret. Why didn't Grandpa like Dad?'

'He's an actor, and he's poor, and he's Jewish.' Noel was surprised to find he was quite sure of this, even though no one had ever said it in front of him. Perhaps there were some things you knew without being told. He said, 'None of these things are important to any sensible person, but I don't know about Grandpa.' He saw him in his mind's eye, red-faced and bellowing. 'I should think he likes things his own way.'

'He's a bully,' Clara said, setting her jaw, looking forward to fighting him.

'He's rich,' Bosie said, very respectfully.

'Greedy,' Clara said. 'That's what you are. Greedy Bosie, always looking for hand-outs.'

'People at school used to have grandparents who gave them nice presents,' Bosie said. 'Birthdays and Christmas and in-between presents.'

'I shouldn't expect them from Grandpa and Liz,' Noel said. 'They've got to feed us and pay for us. Everything costs a lot nowadays.'

He thought of the last, awful few weeks before Dad saw the doctor and went into hospital. The bills coming in, and the mortgage, and Dad sitting slumped in a chair, hands over his face, defeated and weeping. Noel said, 'Even without us, Grandpa must have a lot of expenses. It's a huge house.'

They turned to look at it. When they arrived last night it had been dark. They had been aware of the heavy bulk of the house looming up and around them, but although later on Grandpa had taken Bosie round the back to put his bike in the garage, all Noel and Clara had seen of the outside had been the steps leading up to the front door and the crouching stone lions that flanked them. Now they saw the two handsome wings jutting out either side, three storeys high, with tall windows on two floors and small ones at the top, behind a low parapet. Some of the windows had white wooden shutters fastened across inside the glass. They made the house look empty. Locked up to keep burglars out. Or to keep people in. Like a prison.

'I don't suppose they use all the rooms,' Noel said. 'Just two people.'

For some reason he found he was whispering. And felt shivery suddenly. Perhaps it was the lonely look of the house, surrounded by the tall trees of the overgrown garden, no other houses in sight. Or just the cold, still, lowering day; a silent, grey, woolly sky, and no sun.

Bosie said, whispering too, 'Don't be scared, Noel. It makes *me* feel scarey.' He moved close to his brother and said in a hoarse little voice, 'I was scared in the night. There's a cupboard in my room full of newspapers tied up in bundles, and I can't shut the door. I tried, but the newspapers kept pushing it open. And there's an old rocking horse and it's horribly creaky. It creaked in the night. I woke up and thought someone was riding it. Then I thought something worse. I thought – perhaps it used to be Mum's rocking horse when she was a little girl, and it knew she'd come back, and wanted to see her!'

'Silly dope,' Clara said. 'Dummy.'

Noel put his arm round him. 'If you don't want to sleep by yourself, I expect they'll let you sleep with Clara or me. I'll ask, if you like. I'm sure Liz won't mind. I think she's quite nice.'

'Quite nice for a lizard,' Bosie said, giggling. Even though his fears were real while they lasted, they didn't last long once he'd told someone about them. 'The Lizard,' he said now, his night terrors forgotten. 'That's what I'm going to call her.'

'You mustn't,' Noel said. 'Mum was right. It's unkind.'

'He won't say it in front of her,' Clara said. 'For God's sake, Noel, he isn't a baby. And I don't want him sleeping in my room, keeping me awake with his snuffling. Crawling into my bed when he's had a bad dream and making me go to the lavatory with him in case snakes slither up from the bowl and sink poisoned fangs in his bottom.'

'That's not fair! I never said about snakes in the night time! I never sit on the seat then, I only just go to *pee*!'

'Well, witches with black wings coming out of the cistern. Whatever it is, you're not really frightened. You just make it up because you want company. And *I* want to be private. I wish I could have one of those rooms right at the top. Right away from the pair of you.'

'You wouldn't be private there long,' Noel said. 'Grandpa's got this friend David coming. He said he could sleep in the attic.'

'How do you know he's a friend?' Bosie said, unexpectedly. 'It didn't sound like it at breakfast.'

Clara scowled. 'That's another hateful thing about grown-ups. Carrying on a conversation as if children weren't there. As if we were part of the furniture. Deaf chairs and deaf tables. Not bothering to explain. I mean, if we did it, talking about someone they didn't know, they'd say we were rude. God in Heaven!'

'Don't swear,' Noel said. 'You know what Mum said.'

'Saying "God in Heaven" isn't swearing. It's a prayer.'

'Not the way that you say it.'

'Don't you boss me about, teaching me manners. Mum said that too, didn't she? "Don't be too good and show up the others!"'

'Shut up.'

'Prig. Goody-goody. Noel the Saint.'

'Shut up, *shut up*, Clara.' He turned on her, sick and miserable, shouting at the top of his voice, not caring if anyone heard him. 'I hate you, I really do, just at this moment I *loathe* you.'

Sometimes, if you shouted at Clara, it stopped her. It stopped her now. She went white as paper. 'Don't. Please, Noel. I didn't mean it.'

Bosie said, 'You shouldn't say things you don't mean. And I don't snuffle at night. Only if I have a cold. I'm getting one now hanging round with you fighting. You give me a pain. I'm going to ask if I can have a ride on my bike.'

He ran off towards the house, hop, skip and jump. Liz opened the front door as if she had been looking out for him from a window, the black dog on guard beside her. She bent down to Bosie. They saw her put out her hand to him.

'He'll be OK,' Clara said gloomily. 'You know what he's like. Suck up to anyone when it suits him. I wish I was still young.'

'You're not old. Only twelve.'

'Too old to be sweet.' She chewed on a strand of hair. It was always hard for her to apologize. She had to screw herself up to it. She said, in the end, with a sigh, 'I didn't mean to be beastly. It was Bosie acting scared, not really meaning it, just getting attention. It started me off feeling properly frightened. What you said to Mum was quite true. We've been dumped here with strangers. Not that I'm frightened of them, not exactly. I mean, I don't think they'll beat us or starve us.'

'Or suck our blood?' Noel said, very seriously. 'I don't think – I can't be sure, mind – but I don't *think* they're vampires.'

Clara smiled, but only briefly, as a politeness, and that made him feel foolish. Cracking silly jokes when he knew perfectly well what she meant.

He said, 'It'll be all right once we've been here a day or two. Got to know them. It's only not knowing that's frightening.'

CHAPTER
3

By the evening of that first day they had a better idea of what they were in for. Or thought they had, anyway.

'I quite like it here,' Bosie said, riding the creaking old rocking horse, feet in the worn leather stirrups, hands on the red, wooden mane. 'Better than home, with Dad moaning and groaning. I know he was ill and couldn't help crying, but it did get a bit boring.'

Noel and Clara, on their knees in front of the cupboard in Bosie's bedroom, trying to pack the bundles of yellowing newspapers tighter so that the door wouldn't creep open and scare him, sat back on their heels and looked at each other. Cold-hearted Bosie! But he had only said what they both secretly felt, so they didn't reproach him. All Noel said was, 'Just don't say that to Grandpa. I mean, not the bit about Dad. Grandpa would think he was feeble.'

Bosie rocked the horse faster. 'You don't need to tell me. I know about Grandpa!'

Soon after their mother had left, he had fallen off his bike, on the gravel, and bawled like a calf. 'Stop that noise, Ambrose,' Grandpa had shouted – so loudly and sternly that he had stopped Bosie mid-wail. And though his cut knee had hurt even more when Grandpa had bathed it, picking out the small chips of stone with hard, chilly fingers while Liz hovered, distracted and anxious, with disinfectant and bandages, Bosie had endured the pain silently. 'Good lad,' Grandpa had said when it was over. 'Keep a stiff upper lip, that's the ticket. You're a man. Remember that, Ambrose. Only girls cry.'

'Not *this* girl. I never cry!' Clara said, her eyes smouldering, but Grandpa merely nodded absently, only half hearing her. He had set ideas about children. Good manners were important for both boys and girls; standing up when grown-ups came into the room and doing what they were told, when they were told, 'at the double'. But only boys had to be brave. Boys didn't cry. Or do 'women's work'. Later on, finding Bosie making a cake in the kitchen, expertly beating up egg whites, he watched him with a grimly astonished expression.

'Who set you on to that caper?' he growled, as Bosie folded the snowy froth into the rest of the mixture.

'Liz said I could make a cake as a treat because I'd hurt my poor knee.'

Grandpa's stiff, speckly eyebrows shot up. 'Funny sort of treat for a boy.'

'Oh, I like cooking,' Bosie said. 'When Mum and Dad were both working, I used to cook supper for when they came back from the theatre. Casseroles and jacket pota-toes I could leave in the oven. And when we had lodgers to help with the mortgage, I used to cook for them sometimes.' He smiled at Grandpa with pride. 'My dad says I've got natural talent. I'm going to be a chef when I grow up.'

'Good grief!' Grandpa said. The red lumps on his cheeks darkened to crimson. He looked at Clara and Noel who were waiting for Bosie to finish so they could lick out the bowl. 'And what about you two? Going on the stage, are you? Or taking up dressmaking?'

Clara said, 'I'm going to be a lawyer. Or perhaps a politician. Not a back bencher, though. I'd want to be someone important and powerful, like a Prime Minister. But I haven't made up my mind yet.'

'Hmph,' Grandpa said. 'Well, you've plenty of time.' But he was looking at Noel.

Noel said, 'I think I'd like to go into a bank. I'm quite good at figures. But I don't really mind, so long as I can work in the day time and come home at night to be with my family.'

He had been thinking about this for a long time. Their old house, rented to strangers until Dad was better, backed on to the railway line. Last summer, swinging on the fence in the evenings, watching the trains from the city curve round the bend, through the cutting, he had imagined himself a grown man, walking home from the station, his children running to meet him. No faces or names, just little kids, three or four of them, holding their arms up, eager for kisses, for him to carry them up to bed, read them stories.

A safe, happy dream he had kept to himself, very private, but now, with Grandpa's baffled gaze bent upon him, he felt deeply uncomfortable. If Grandpa had guessed, he would surely despise him, bark at him angrily. 'A children's nurse! Is that all you want to be? God Almighty!'

But his grandfather said, with sudden, surprising gentleness, 'Well, that fits, I suppose. In the circumstances.'

When he had left the kitchen, Clara said, 'Oh, you are a slimy creep, Noel! Making him pity us! Poor little children, left alone every night, having to cook their own supper, put themselves to bed, wicked parents out at the theatre.'

'That's not fair. I didn't mean it like that and you know it. So did he, I expect. He knows Mum and Dad have to work in the evenings. It's their job, being actors.'

'Not a man's job, though.' Clara giggled. 'Not according to Grandpa. I should think you'd have to be a soldier to please him. Something rough and tough, real hard, dangerous work, like being on an oil rig, or a coal miner.'

'Or a racing driver,' Bosie said. 'If I get bored with cooking, I think that's what I'd like to be.'

Grandpa had been a soldier, fighting in two World Wars, but he had never worked on an oil rig, or down a coal mine. As a boy, leaving school at eleven he had worked for a milkman in the East End of London, getting up at half past four in the morning, helping to push the milk cart and ladle the milk from the churns into cans. After the first war he had earned his living as a mechanic, taken exams at night school, saved his wages, and after the second war he had started his own motor-bike factory and made a fortune.

'Pulled myself up by my boot straps,' he told the children. 'Started with nothing except my two hands, owed nothing to nobody, never out of work during the Depression. Hard work and character, that's the right ticket.'

Even when they had heard this so often they could have

24

said the words for him, they listened respectfully. He wasn't boasting, they decided, just telling them what his life had been like, making up for all the years he'd not known them. And although it was tedious, sometimes, hearing the same thing over and over, and he could still alarm them by a sudden, barking command or an outburst of temper, they soon knew more or less how to treat him. After his midday nap was an angry time, and it was best to keep quiet then, keep away from the front hall and the door of his study, and go to their rooms by the narrow back stair that led up from the wash room behind the kitchen. He was old, he was crotchety, but so were lots of grandfathers in the books they had read, and they felt fairly comfortable with him.

They were much less comfortable with Liz. Even though she was kind, producing books and games that had belonged to their mother out of an old chest in the attic, and letting Bosie make cakes when he wanted, she never stayed to play a game with them, never talked, never asked questions. She was all angles and nerves and so shy, perferring to talk to the dog, to old, half blind Nero, than directly to people. Perhaps she was just being shy to begin with, as their mother had said she might be, but it made them uneasy. They called her 'The Lizard' but she was more like the ghost of one, scared by its own meagre shadow.

But just when it began to seem there was nothing more to her – or, if there was, that she didn't want them to know it – she flew into a passionate rage with Mrs Battle, the housekeeper, and accused her of stealing.

CHAPTER

4

Mrs Battle came four days a week, Tuesday to Friday, arriving at ten in the morning in a bright red new Volkswagen and leaving at six. She cooked lunch for the children, eating with them in the kitchen while Grandpa and Liz had sandwiches and milk in the study, and laid a cold supper for them all in the dining room. She was a tall, heavy woman with a fuzz of red hair in tight curls and large, gleaming eyes that were the pale grey of fish scales. She showed a lot of pink gum when she laughed, which was often, though not always when something was funny.

She laughed when she first met the children, displaying her gums and a flash of gold in her back teeth.

'We'll get along, don't you worry,' she said when Liz introduced them. 'Extra work, naturally, but that's never worried me. As long as I get no complaints about other things being skimped. I've only two hands, you know.'

Liz, standing in the kitchen doorway with Nero beside her, touched the dog's head. 'Not many people have more than two hands, Mrs Battle. And I don't think I've ever complained. Your work has always been satisfactory.'

Her voice was unusually clipped and clear, but as soon as she'd spoken she darted away, the dog padding after her, and Mrs Battle winked at the children. 'My, my,' she said. 'On our hind legs this morning, aren't we? Quite the duchess. How are you getting on with your grandmother? Bit sharp with you, is she?'

'Not at all, Mrs Battle,' Clara said, rather stiffly. 'We get on very well with her, thank you.'

'Call me Batty, dear,' Mrs Battle said. 'Don't be formal. Start as you mean to go on and I like to be friendly.'

'Batty!' Bosie squealed suddenly, doubling up as if he had a pain in his stomach. 'Our father is *batty*. Gone crazy!'

'Now, now,' Mrs Battle said. 'That's not a nice thing for a little boy to say about his poor daddy.'

But she was smiling. Bosie turned scarlet.

'He's had a nervous breakdown, that's what Bosie means,' Noel said quickly, feeling embarrassed because a nervous breakdown didn't seem like a real illness, somehow. Not something you could talk about, like appendicitis, or measles. He was sorry for his father, but a bit ashamed, too.

Mrs Battle pulled her face straight. It seemed an effort for her to look solemn. She said, 'Oh, dear me, nerves are a terrible thing. Once you've started, you never really get rid of them. Your poor grandmother suffers, you know. I have to remind myself, because she's not easy to work for. Many a time I've said to myself – "That's enough, Batty, you don't have to take it!" But then I think, poor old soul, how will she manage? If I give in my notice, who will step in? Your grandparents aren't popular, I'm afraid, down the village. Too much of *this* . . .' She pressed a finger on the end of her nose and tilted it upwards. 'Think they're too good for the rest of us, that's my meaning. Though as I tell everyone, they're just old, if they want to keep themselves to themselves, it isn't a crime.' She gave one of her pink, gummy laughs. 'Big-hearted Batty, that's me!'

She sang round the house as she worked, making a noisy clatter with brooms and pans, leaving little puddles of dirty water on the tiled floor of the hall, energetically polished furniture with a frayed, greasy rag. 'Just a lick and a promise,' she cried, bursting into the children's rooms and whirling round with an old vacuum cleaner that seemed to puff out more dust than it ever sucked in. She was rough and ready but she seemed jolly enough, quite friendly and kind, until the day that Liz lost a pot of face cream, and her temper.

That was on Friday. The fish van came Fridays, and Mrs Battle had made a flaky fish pie. She was a better cook than she was a cleaner and they were finishing their second big helpings when Liz flung open the door of the kitchen.

For once the dog wasn't with her. She was breathless with agitation, her bony chest heaving, her lined face twitching restlessly. 'Why did you steal it?' she shouted, in a harsh, angry voice. 'Tell me at once, Mrs Battle. What have you done with it?'

'Are you calling me a thief?' Mrs Battle said calmly, not moving from her place at the table. 'You'll be sorry for that, later on. What am I supposed to have stolen?'

'My face cream. A large pot with a gold lid.' Liz wrung her small hands. 'It's not where I left it.'

'And where was that, dear?' Mrs Battle smiled – a small secretive smile, slightly sneering. 'Or can't you remember?'

'Of course I remember,' Liz wailed – frenzied now, on the verge of tears. 'I've been looking and looking.'

'Look a bit longer, and I dare say you'll find it,' Mrs Battle said. 'Unless the fairies have taken it.'

She winked at the children as if she were sharing a private joke with them. Liz gave a strangled cry and ran from the kitchen.

Bosie laughed. It was only nervousness, but Clara looked at him sharply. She said, 'Bosie! Have you been up to something?'

He shook his head. Mrs Battle said, 'She's always losing things. Lose her own head one day. Why turn on your poor little brother?'

'Oh, I steal sometimes,' Bosie said cheerfully. 'I mean, I used to when I was young. I used to take things that I needed. But I don't need face cream.'

'Nor does she,' Mrs Battle said. 'Fat lot of good face cream will do her. I've seen her, laying it on, hoping for miracles. Vain, silly old woman.'

Although it did seem ridiculous, the idea of the Lizard anointing her dry, wrinkled skin, as if she could smooth it out and make it young again, the children looked down at their plates without smiling. When they looked up, Mrs Battle was laughing, her pale eyes rolling in their sockets like wet, shiny pebbles. 'Come on, now! Don't look so miserable. Old people are full of stupid fancies, they fly off the handle one minute and forget it the next. Best thing is to do what I do, and pay no attention.'

They were almost convinced. But after lunch, when they had finished their ice cream dessert and gone quietly up the back stairs as usual, they stood on the landing and listened. They could hear Grandpa snoring downstairs in his study, a low, steady rumble, punctuated with little sharp snorts. And, from Liz's bedroom, small sighs and whimpers. They stood outside, hesitating.

Clara whispered, 'We could help her look. D'you think we should, Noel?'

He went reluctantly into the room, Clara and Bosie behind him. Liz was sitting at her dressing table, looking at her face in the mirror. It was a theatrical mirror, with lit, naked bulbs all around it, and in this clear, unshadowed light, Noel could see why he had thought, when he first saw her, that she was like a lizard. She had almost no eyebrows or eyelashes and without them her dark eyes looked skinned.

She didn't seem surprised to see Noel. She blinked at him in the glass and said, with quiet desperation, 'I know I'm old but I'm not senile yet. The jar was here, in front of the mirror this morning. I didn't move it. But *she*'s been here, cleaning. Or what she calls cleaning.'

'Perhaps she tidied it up,' Noel said. 'Put it some other place when she was dusting.'

He couldn't think where. The room was a mess, clothes scattered on the chairs, on the floor, on the rumpled bed where Nero lay sleeping, and all the drawers open, spilling out silk scarves and fur tippets and stockings and underwear, as if Liz had been scrabbling frantically through them.

Bosie and Clara began picking up clothes, looking under the bed, in the cupboards. Noel went into the bathroom. The bath had a grubby line round it but the floor was still damp and a smelly, wet mop, leaning against the wall by the basin, suggested that Mrs Battle had been here.

Noel looked vaguely round, wondering. There was nothing in the medicine cabinet but bottles of pills and a tooth mug, and on the shelf over the bath, soap and lavatory paper. But the shelf was deep. When he climbed on the rim of the bath and moved a packet of Kleenex, he saw the jar at the back. A squat glass jar with a gold, screwtop lid.

He jumped down, feeling triumphant. Although it was silly of Liz to make such a fuss about a small thing, it clearly wasn't a small thing to her.

He ran to the bedroom. 'Is this it? I found it on the shelf.'

'Oh!' She held it in her hands for a moment before she put it down on the dressing table. 'Thank you, Noel, how silly of me, I must have left it there and forgotten.' She smiled up at him. 'I'm a foolish, forgetful old woman.'

Something was puzzling him. Flitting about on the edge of his mind. He couldn't quite pin it down. He said, 'It was right at the back of the shelf. You couldn't have reached it.'

Then the truth hit him. She was too frail and shaky to climb on the edge of the bath. He saw that her hands were shaking now, clasped in her lap and guessed why. He said, shocked, 'It was tucked away. *Hidden.*'

She sighed. She said in a soft, ashamed voice, 'Mrs Battle hides my things sometimes. She likes to make me seem stupid.' She gave a little, forced laugh and looked beyond Noel, at Bosie, who was staring, round-eyed. 'Don't look so startled, dear. All's well that ends well. It's just a game she plays sometimes.'

'I don't think it's a game,' Clara said. 'I think it's most terribly mean. A person who could do something like that is rotten right to the core. I'm going straight down to tell her we've found it.'

'No,' Liz said. 'Please.' She put out her hand as if to touch Clara, then let it fall to her lap. She said, 'She'll leave

31

if we say anything to upset her, and what would we do then? When we bought this house, just after the war, when your mother was little, we had two maids and a gardener. But now times have changed and it's hard to get help, a place this size, so far from the village. No one else would come if she left, all the other women she knows make much more money at the frozen food factory.'

'That's what *she* tells you,' Clara said hotly.

'It may be true, dear. Even if it isn't, your grandfather wouldn't want someone new. He doesn't like change.'

Bosie said, 'If Grandpa knew she was horrible to you, he'd put a stop to it. He'd be terribly angry.'

'That's why he mustn't know, Bosie. It's bad for him to get angry, it puts up his blood pressure. Besides, he'd be angry with *me*, for being such an old silly! I get so stupidly fussed when I lose things.' She caught her breath and looked grave. 'I shouldn't have accused her of stealing!'

'She did steal in a way,' Noel said. 'She took your face cream and hid it.'

'That was just teasing, dear. If I hadn't lost my temper, she'd have put it back later on, without saying anything.'

She sounded quite composed now, as if that was all that had happened. She had been an 'old silly' because she had forgotten the rules of the game that Mrs Battle played with her. A weird game. A cruel game . . .

Clara said, 'Taking things and hiding them and pretending you haven't is frightening. She frightened you.'

She said – apologetically, as if this was *her* fault, 'Well, a bit, perhaps. It's part of getting old, really. You get old, you get frightened, most of the time for no reason.'

The children looked at her. Bosie said, 'Are you frightened of us? I mean, *were* you frightened? When we first came.'

32

She regarded him seriously. 'No, I don't think so. Only worried that you might not like me. I thought – my grandchildren coming, what will they think when they see this little, old scrumpled-up creature!'

She gave a sudden, bright, merry laugh, and they saw that before her skin crinkled up, she must have been pretty. She had a small face with a short nose and a delicate cleft in her chin. A little like Clara, Noel thought, surprised; like Clara grown old, and without her fierce look.

Liz said, 'I'm a vain woman, as I daresay Mrs Battle has told you. She tells me often enough! Though it wasn't just vanity. I was afraid you'd be so unhappy here on your own, away from your mother, having to go to new schools and live with two tiresome old people. I don't know much about children. Your mother was our only child and we had a nurse for her when she was little. I was nearly forty when she was born, and your grandfather thought it would tire me to look after a baby. He liked me to dress up and look pretty and young and I wanted to please him. He was always so good to me . . .'

She smiled absently, as if she had slipped back to the past, far away from them. 'I was an actress, a chorus girl, when he met me, and that's a hard life, singing and dancing, once you're past your first youth. That's why Grandpa didn't want your mother to go on the stage, or marry an actor, he'd hoped for a better life for her, but she was a match for him, determined to do what she wanted. Such a wilful girl, full of temper . . .'

'It's the artistic temperament,' Noel said, afraid she was criticizing.

'Oh, I know, dear. But hard to live with sometimes.' She looked at him mischievously. 'Grandpa and your mother used to be at it, hammer and tongs, too much alike

33

to get on, that was really the trouble, and I'd creep away to my room and put on the gramophone and dance all alone until they had finished. I like peace in a house.'

She pulled a wry face, screwing up her small nose like a little girl who knew she'd been naughty but was pleased with herself all the same. 'That's why I must go to Mrs Battle and say that I'm sorry I called her a thief. Otherwise there will be tantrums and a badly cooked supper. Not that I mind for myself, I eat like a bird, always have done, that's how I've kept myself trim, but Grandpa would grumble, and you children like your food, don't you? I know David eats like a horse.'

She turned on the stool to look in the glass and picked up a powder puff, fluffing it over her face until the powder lay in pale drifts in the wrinkles, humming a little tune under her breath as if it helped her to concentrate. She dabbed a patch of rouge on each cheekbone, a bright, scarlet penny, drew a lipstick bow on her thin, upper lip and a brown pencil line where her eyebrows would be if she had them. And, when she had finished, she smiled at her reflection as if she felt tender towards it.

The children felt awkward – out of place and forgotten. Only Bosie had the courage to ask what they all wanted to know. 'Who's David?' he said, as she stood up, smoothing her skirt down, and taking a last look in the mirror.

Perhaps she didn't hear him. Or didn't want to. She clicked her fingers and said, 'Come on, Nero, come and help Mother eat humble pie, will you, old fellow?'

Nero rose on the bed and jumped heavily down. The painted old woman and the stiff-legged old dog walked side by side to the door. 'Is David coming to supper?' Bosie asked as they reached it, but though she did hear this time, heard him speak, anyway, because she turned smiling sweetly, she didn't answer.

34

'Potty,' Clara said when she was out of earshot. 'Quite potty.'

'No she isn't,' Noel said. 'She just flips a bit. Her mind hops about. She's just old.'

'I didn't mean *she* was potty,' Clara said. 'I meant, the whole thing! The whole, potty scene!'

'It was Batty's fault,' Bosie said. 'It's Batty who's *batty*!' He pulled an idiot face, crossing his eyes and dropping his jaw, his healthy pink tongue loose and slobbering.

'If you make that joke again, even *once* more, I'll stitch your mouth up,' Clara said. But this horrid threat had no heat behind it. She went on, frowning and thoughtful. 'And I didn't really mean *potty*, either. It was the first word that came but it doesn't fit, somehow. It's – oh, I don't know – too sort of pretty . . .'

'Pretty potty,' Bosie said, sniggering.

'Don't be feeble,' Noel said. 'You want something serious. Heavier. A bit darker.'

They considered words. The shape and the sound and the meaning. *Bank* and *Bill* were hard words, like hammers. *Lewd* was wriggly and funny. *Summer* was happy, like *Singing* and *Picnic*. There were safe words and brave words and words full of danger. They wanted a dangerous word for what had happened just now, for the extraordinary way Mrs Battle had treated their grandmother, playing silly tricks, sneering, taunting her because she was old and forgot things. *Potty* was quite the wrong word for that sort of spiteful behaviour. It was too cheerful and tripping; a light, harmless word.

It was Bosie who thought of the right one. It formed in his mind thin, black and snaky. '*Sinister*,' he said, liking the hiss of it, and the cold, slithery feeling it gave him. 'That old Batty is sinister!'

CHAPTER

5

Bosie was more on his own than the others. Noel and Clara had been alive before he was born and for them he would always be odd one out, Bosie-the-Baby. This was what he felt, anyway, and he resented it sometimes. Ten wasn't so much younger than twelve and fourteen; the trouble was, he could never catch up. It seemed that whatever he did they had already done, been there before him.

It made him a bit secretive. Exploring the house alone, getting up with the sleepy birds at first light, he was careful not to wake Noel and Clara, and some things he discovered he kept to himself, close and private. He didn't tell them about the nest of mice he found in the old sofa. Nor about the gun in the attic.

Dawn was just before seven these cold February mornings. Bosie, pulling on jeans and sweater and padding in his socks from his room to the landing, heard the hoarse whirr as the clock in the hall below got ready to strike. No other sound except Grandpa snoring – different snores from his midday nap, the steady snores of deep sleep, solemn and rolling.

Bosie enjoyed the feeling that the house belonged to him, a whole hour before anyone stirred, before Liz's alarm went off at eight and she went down to the kitchen in gold slippers and red silk kimono to make morning tea and let the dog out in the garden. He enjoyed being alone in the large, unused, shuttered room on the first floor where dusty chandeliers hung from the ceiling and the shrouded furniture seemed to float like pale, ghostly islands in the creepy half-dark. He peeped under the covers to find heavy, old-fashioned arm chairs, pulled faces at his dim reflection in the huge, spotted mirrors with carved, golden frames, and lifted the lid of the grand piano to touch the yellowing keys. It must have been a room for parties, he thought, a ballroom, but now it smelled musty and dusty, the pretty clocks under glass bells that stood on the two marble mantelpieces had stopped long ago, and one sofa, patterned with faded blue peacocks, had a nest of mice in it. He heard something squeaking, and when he lifted the dust sheet, little, black shining eyes looked at him brightly. They didn't seem frightened, perhaps he was the first human being they'd seen, and he remembered stories of prisoners who fed the mice in their cells and made friends of them. 'Don't worry,' he whispered, 'I won't tell anyone. If you'll be friends with me, I'll bring you some biscuits.'

Although he liked the mice and the ballroom, he liked the attic rooms best because there was more to see there. He poked about in tin trunks with tarnished brass clasps, and in camphor wood chests, full of clothes that he decided must belong to his grandmother. There were cracked shoes with high, narrow heels and sharp points to the toes, stiff, taffeta petticoats, fur wraps smelling of moth balls that had horrid animal heads with bead eyes dangling from them, and bright, slippery dresses. In one of the trunks there were theatre programmes, bound up with rotting silk ribbons, and in another, a lot of brown photographs of bearded men with fierce faces and ladies in high-buttoned blouses. He found an old straw hat labelled DEAR FATHER'S GARDENING HAT, half a dozen pairs of rusty skates in a cupboard and a harmonium that wheezed when he pumped the pedals, like an ancient man with bronchitis.

There were five attics, all leading into each other, but only one that was properly furnished for someone to sleep in – an iron-frame bed, a chest of drawers, rugs on the floor, and a rocking chair with a tapestry seat. There was a dolls' house in this room, too, and a big, roll-top desk. The dolls' house was locked, the hasp at the side secured by a small padlock, but the desk was open. Bosie thought it was empty at first, nothing in the pigeon holes except dust and a few paper clips, until he discovered the flat, sliding partition. It was stiff and he had to poke and prod with the point of his knife before he could budge it. The cavity beneath was crammed full of old papers, letters and old documents written in black ink on thick paper, none of which looked very interesting, and, right at the bottom, the gun.

It was in a brown leather holster. Bosie took it out carefully. He had never seen a real gun before, a revolver, and he played with it, aiming at the pigeons that strutted on the parapet outside the window, and pretending to be a bank robber, pulling the collar of his sweater up to cover the lower part of his face and hissing, 'Hand over the money or I'll shoot daylight through you.' Then he wondered if the gun was loaded. He didn't know how to find out and he was afraid it might go off by accident, so he put it back in the holster and hid it where he had found it, under the papers. He closed the partition and the roll top of the desk, feeling excited and furtive. Clara and Noel would say he'd been nosy, looking through Grandpa's desk, Grandpa's papers. Nosy-Bosie. Well, he wouldn't give them the pleasure. He wouldn't tell them he'd found Grandpa's gun.

Was it Grandpa's gun? The gun he had had in the war when he'd been a soldier? Had he killed someone with it? The war had been over a long time, forty years, nearly. If Grandpa had put the gun away in the desk all that time ago, he had probably forgotten by now. The thought that he was the only one who knew it was there made Bosie shiver a little, quite pleasantly.

'Sinister,' he said to himself on Saturday morning, pleased to find another use for this good, slithery word as he stood outside the house, looking up at the attic and thinking of the gun, the instrument of death hidden there. *Bosie's sinister secret.*

Rain had kept him indoors all the week. But it had turned cold and dry in the night and the grass bristled with hairy frost that squeaked under his feet as he pushed his way through the tangled garden, through the thickets of saplings that had grown up round the trees. Away from the lawn and the bed of rose bushes that Liz still kept weeded, whippy branches closed over his head and behind him, and beneath the crisp, frosty surface, the ground was soggy with rotting leaves. Almost like being lost in a wild wood, he thought, not a garden, until he came upon a little

39

glade, with a statue of a naked girl, clothed with dark, spotted ivy, and a pair of tall, iron gates just beyond her.

The gates were locked but there was no fence or lawn either side and so he went round them, finding a narrow path that sloped sharply down into a deep, overgrown dell. He slipped on the path, on icy mud, trying to hold on to the brambles that flicked his face, and slid down, scratched and dirty, to a brown, silted-up pond at the bottom, with a dead tree lying across it.

He stood on the damp, reedy edge of the pond, and looked up. Trees hid the sky and almost concealed a small house high up on the other side of the dell. He crossed the pond, balancing on the dead tree, and climbed up. There were a few rough wooden steps, but it was still a steep climb and by the time he reached the little house he was panting.

It was a summer house with a porch that faced down into the dell. Once, perhaps, people had sat here, enjoying the view, but now the basket chairs were filthy and sagging, the wood floor was rotten, and even the lacy iron steps were broken in places. No one could have been here for ages and ages, Bosie thought, holding his breath as he pushed at the door. He must be the first person in years . . .

But he wasn't. Someone else was already there. Someone sleeping on an old couch, under a blanket, only the top of a curly head visible at one end, and a pair of boots at the other.

Terror closed Bosie's throat. Just a tramp, he told himself bravely, a poor old tramp, dossed down for the night. Stepping backwards, trying to close the door silently, he stumbled against one of the chairs on the porch and the sleeper sat up with a grunt, shaking back thick, dark hair, staring at Bosie. A young man with a plump, pink-

and-white face, blue eyes with long lashes and a very red, pouting mouth. Not a tramp, Bosie thought – too young and too clean. And with that rather babyish, pretty face, not at all frightening.

He said, 'I'm sorry I woke you up. What are you doing here?'

'I could ask you that,' the man said. 'Bursting in without knocking.' He sounded aggrieved.

'I live here,' Bosie said. 'I mean, I live in the house. With my grandparents. This is their summer house.'

He looked round him. Swags of dark cobwebs hung from the ceiling and green mould grew on the walls. Apart from the couch, and a couple of croquet mallets propped up in one corner, the small room was empty.

Bosie said, 'They don't use it, they're too old, that's why it's so dirty. I suppose you thought it didn't belong to anyone so it was all right to sleep here. But it is private property.'

The man pushed back the blanket. He swung his legs over the side of the couch and stood up, stretching his arms high above his head, yawning hugely. His sweater rose up as he stretched, exposing a large expanse of very white skin and a very pink navel. When he put his arms down, his navel disappeared in a crease, and his belly rolled over the belt of his jeans. He tugged at his sweater and patted his stomach.

He said, 'I'm not trespassing, Ambrose. Just being considerate. The truck dropped me off in the village at three in the morning and I didn't want to wake everyone up. That sort of thing starts you off on the wrong foot. You are Ambrose, aren't you?'

'Only Grandpa calls me that. Everyone else calls me Bosie. How do you know who I am?'

'Oh, I know a lot of things. This one was easy. You're

41

the younger boy, aren't you?' Through his long lashes the fat young man's eyes sparkled like water with the sun shining on it. 'You see? I know about you but you don't know about me. You've been kept in the dark!'

Bosie understood suddenly. 'You're David. Grandpa said David was coming!'

He laughed. 'Bet that's all he said, though! Sly old fox. Still, it'll do for a start. How are the old folks? And how's Batty? Good old Batty! She'll be pleased to see me even if they aren't so keen.'

'I don't know. I expect so,' Bosie said, feeling confused.

David looked at him, smiling with some private amusement. 'Never mind. You and I will be chums, won't we, Bosie? Help me tidy up, for a start.'

He didn't need help. Although he looked big and clumsy, his movements were quick and efficient, folding the blanket, tying it with two leathers straps and fastening it to a long canvas kitbag that he slung over his shoulder. He picked his jacket up from the couch and banged at the shabby cushions, raising a whirlwind of dust that made them both cough.

'This place needs a good clean,' David said in a disgusted voice as they escaped from the dusty room and stood on the porch. 'And not just the summer house.' He waved a hand at the dell. 'Look at that jungle! There used to be moorhens come to nest on that pond, now it stinks like a sewer. I could clean it out, fix it up, the big house as well as the garden, if only they'd let me. But it's always excuses, excuses. That's the trouble with elderly people, they let things slide until it's all rack and ruin. They don't seem to realize they should protect their investment. It's selfishness, really! They think *they* won't need it much longer, so why should they bother?'

His pink-and-white face had turned broody and sullen

42

and he seemed to be talking more to himself than to Bosie, who was watching him shyly, wondering what he had meant by 'investment' but not liking to ask while David was looking so angry. Instead, he said, 'If you want to clean out the pond, I could help you. I'm stronger than I look and I don't mind getting muddy.'

David looked at him then and smiled slowly. 'That's not a bad idea, Bosie. Might be better if it comes from you, though. Tell you what, I'll pick the right moment, you make the suggestion. Right?'

'Right,' Bosie said, a bit doubtfully.

David hit him playfully on the shoulder. 'You're *on*, boy,' he said. 'You and me will make a good team. Let's get going.'

Bosie followed him round the back of the summer house where there was a better path than the steep, slippery way up from the pond. It led through a shrubbery of towering old rhododendrons to the main drive, by the gate. 'I never knew the summer house was there till this morning,' Bosie said. 'You can't see it from the house. Only from down in the dell.'

'Very useful, that,' David said. 'To tell you the truth I often camp there without letting them know. I like to keep an eye on things. I reckon someone ought to do that when people get old.' He glanced at Bosie and his expression was suddenly a bit sharp, a bit sly. 'That's a secret I'm telling you, mind! I wouldn't want the old folks to think I was spying. Though they'd be glad enough to have me close by if something did happen. If there was a fire, or if one of them fell down in a fit.'

How would David know, Bosie thought, hidden out of sight in the summer house? Still, it was kind of him to worry about Grandpa and Liz. Bosie said, 'Of course I won't tell them.'

'Good man,' David said. 'Keep it under your hat.'

They walked towards the house. Liz was at the open front door, wearing her red silk kimono, calling her dog. 'Nero. Nero! Come here, old fellow.'

Nero blundered out of the bushes in front of Bosie, banging clumsily against his legs, making him totter. David caught his arm, steadying him, and said, as Nero cantered heavily down the drive, throwing out his back legs, 'Time that old dog was put down! Deaf, almost blind – he could do someone a serious injury.'

'But Liz loves him,' Bosie protested, watching his grandmother bend down to fondle him, taking his head in her hands, murmuring to him. Although she must have seen David and Bosie, she ignored them until they were standing in front of her. Then she looked at David and said, 'Oh, it's you is it?'

It seemed a cold welcome. But David was smiling. He kissed her heartily on both cheeks, making a wet, smacking sound, and said, 'How are you, Grandmother?'

She flinched back, jerking her small body away from him. Her face was wizened and ugly above her beautiful gown. She said, 'How *dare* you call me that, David? How many times do I have to tell you?'

CHAPTER
6

All Clara heard, coming downstairs at that moment, was the tail end of Liz's last sentence and the bitter tone of her voice. She didn't know why Liz was so angry, and, seeing David's hurt face over her grandmother's hunched, bony shoulder, didn't care, either. David had looked like a man to Bosie, but he looked like a boy to her, a big, blushing, vulnerable boy, not much older than she was. She flew to protect him.

'What's the matter? Why are you all standing here in the cold with the door open? Liz, you'll catch your death in that thin kimono. You ought to wear something more sensible these winter mornings.' She smiled brightly at David as if she had only just noticed him. 'Hallo, there! Hi! Why don't you come in?'

Liz turned. She said, cold and controlled now, 'Clara

dear, this is David. I am about to make him some breakfast. Since he has arrived so unsuitably early, we'll
eat in the kitchen. We won't wait for Grandpa and
Noel.'

She pranced off in her silly, pretty, gold slippers and
closed the kitchen door with a bang.

Clara said, laughing, 'Don't pay any attention. She flies
up and down! What got into her *this* time?'

David stepped into the hall, put his kitbag down and
rubbed at his shoulder. His red mouth was trembling. He
said, 'I shouldn't have come. I can see that. I keep hoping
each time, try to please her, but she never gives me a
chance. I don't know what I've done to make her hate me
so much.'

'I'm sure she doesn't hate you,' Clara said, feeling
uncomfortable. However much someone had hurt her,
however bad she was feeling, she would never admit it so
openly. But perhaps it was wrong to be stiff and proud!
David was just a very honest person, she decided, determined to like him.

Bosie said, 'She was only cross because she didn't like
you calling her grandmother. She even makes us call her
Liz, and we're her *grandchildren*!'

David smiled. There was something odd about his
smile, Clara thought. As if he knew something they
didn't. But all he said was, 'Thanks for the advice, you're a
pal, Bosie.'

Bosie wriggled with pleasure. He said, 'Liz really is silly
to mind. Old people are often called Granny or Grandad
by people who aren't their relations. Conductors on buses
say, "Come along, Grandad," when an old man is slow
getting on. It's meant to be friendly.'

David sighed. Clara thought it might make him feel
better if she changed the conversation politely. 'Did you

46

have a good journey?' she asked. 'Did you come by train or by bus?'

'Oh, I can't afford that kind of luxury!' David sounded almost offended, as if Clara ought to have known this. 'I got a lift on a truck. Not the way I would wish to travel, but beggars can't be choosers, you know.'

Clara wondered if he really were poor. 'David's had a rough time,' was what Grandpa had said at breakfast on their first day. But he didn't look like a beggar. He was wearing a good leather jacket with silver studs on the shoulders and his fringed, cowboy boots looked expensive. Perhaps he had used all his money on smart clothes to come on this visit. Hoping to impress Liz. Poor David! She said, 'Are you hungry?'

'What do you think?' He smiled at her properly, a beautiful, full, glowing smile, blue eyes shining.

He certainly ate as if he were famished. Bosie cooked him a second helping of eggs and bacon and he ate almost a whole loaf of bread, wiping his plate so clean it might have come straight from the dishwasher, first with the bread, then with his finger. When he had finished, he sat back and belched. Although it was a delicate belch, and he put his hand over his mouth to conceal it, Clara was glad that Grandpa, with his fixed ideas about table manners, was not there to see.

She said, excusing him, in case Liz disapproved too, 'You must have been *starving*.'

He watched her through his long lashes. 'That was my first meal for a couple of days. Apart from some sandwiches the truck driver gave me. And they tasted of engine oil. I had quite a job getting them down.'

'Well, I expect you'll make up for it now that you're here,' Liz said bracingly. All the time he was eating she

47

had sat sipping her tea, not eating herself, saying nothing. Now she gave him a small, tight smile as if to apologize for her unkindness earlier. 'I'm going to dress now. Bosie, it's almost nine o'clock. I'd be grateful if you would see to breakfast for Grandpa and Noel. I'll call them both when I go upstairs. David, you are to sleep in the attic. Clara will see you have clean sheets and towels. I expect you would like a bath. And, please, David . . .'

She stopped, her mouth twitching.

'Yes?' David said. 'Go on. Please, David – *what*?' Grinning, he put his head on one side. Trying to coax her.

But whatever she had meant to say, she had decided against it. She set her lips in a thin line and tucked her hands inside her kimono sleeves as if she were cold. 'It'll keep,' she said, and looked at him, a long, level look, without blinking.

Clara liked mysteries. But sometimes not knowing was more exciting than finding out. Although she longed to know more about David, she decided not to ask questions just yet. Where had he come from? Once or twice he had spoken like an American. Had he been to America? Clara sat in the rocking chair in the attic hugging the delicious feeling of mystery to her while she watched David unpack. 'A dark stranger,' she told herself, pushing aside the thought that he would be more romantic and mysterious if he were not quite so fat. After all, in spite of his bulk, he was graceful and quick in his movements, light on his feet as a cat or a dancer. The wide old boards of the attic floor barely creaked under his weight as he emptied his kitbag and carefully re-folded his clothes before putting them away in the drawers of the chest.

He hung his jacket on the hook on the back of the door, straightened the bed cover and said, looking round him,

'There we are. Not very grand, but everything ship-shape. I can't stand untidiness.'

'Just as well you're not sleeping with me, then.' Clara spoke without thinking, then felt the embarrassing heat rise up in her face. 'I mean, my room is such a fearful mess always. Bosie is the only tidy one in our family. Do you mind sleeping up here in the attic? Would you rather be on the first floor? There's only one spare room empty, and I expect Liz wants to keep that in case my mother should come, but Bosie could always move in with Noel.'

'Grandmother wouldn't like that,' he said. 'The attic's good enough for David! Servants' quarters. That's where I belong in her opinion.'

'I'm sure that's not true! Really, David! Liz just gave us the best rooms because we came first. And because we're going to be here longer than you are. I mean, you've just come for a *visit*!'

'How do you know?' He smiled at her, his slow, knowing smile. 'If that's what your grandmother thinks, then she may have another think coming!'

It sounded like a threat. Clara said, puzzled, 'I only meant, we have to stay until our father is better, and that may be *months*. We're even going to school here, starting next week. Bosie is going to a school in the village, but Noel and I have to go to the town. It's about eight miles, too far to walk, but Liz says the school bus passes the gate . . .'

Although he nodded, he was not really listening. He was looking at himself in the mirror on top of the chest, frowning at his reflection in a preoccupied way. It made Clara chatter on nervously. 'Of course, Dad may get better sooner than we think, but he may not be well enough to work for a long time. And it's out of sight, out of mind, in the theatre. It was all right when both Mum and Dad were in our local repertory company. But they had a bad season last winter and closed down at the end of the summer.'

David said thoughtfully, still regarding himself in the mirror, arching his neck and jutting his jaw, 'I've sometimes thought of taking up acting. The movies, or television. But it's hard to decide. The trouble is, I'm good at so many things.' He turned from the glass and looked at her. 'You see, I'm a genius, Clara. That makes it difficult for me. If I take up one thing, then I'm wasting my talents in another direction.'

Clara laughed and he looked surprised. She said quickly, 'I'm sorry. It's just, well, I've never heard anyone say he was a genius before.'

'Perhaps I'm the first one you've met. As a matter of fact, I don't usually tell people because it makes them so jealous. You aren't jealous, are you?' He came close to the rocking chair and looked down at her. 'No, of course not. You're not that kind of crude person. In fact, you're unusually sympathetic and sensitive. I knew it as soon as I saw you. I thought – "that's an intelligent and beautiful girl, she'll be on my side, I can trust her." I can trust you, can't I?'

His blue eyes had an intent, burning look. Clara felt hypnotized. She said, in a small weak voice, 'Oh. Oh, yes. Yes, you can.'

He gave a small satisfied nod. 'Good. That's settled then. I may have a lot to put up with, here in this house, but I can bear it now that I know you'll stand up for me.'

He took her hands and pulled her up from the chair. He bent his head until his smooth, pretty face was close to hers. He said, 'Let's seal the bargain,' and kissed her. His lips were soft and a little bit wet. Clara felt his kiss tingle through her. She shivered and tried to pull away but his

50

hands were on her shoulders now, holding her firmly, and it seemed rude to struggle.

She was partly relieved and partly ashamed when Liz said, from the doorway, 'That will do, David.'

Liz was dressed and made up and wearing a ginger wig, all tight curls and rather too big for her. She came into the room, Nero beside her. David let Clara go and turned to her, smiling.

He said, 'What's wrong, Grandma? Just a little kiss between cousins.'

Liz's eyes snapped at him. 'Cousins? I thought you would at least have the decency to keep your mouth shut about that.'

David shrugged his shoulders. 'OK. *OK*. But what harm is there in it? I'm not a monster, am I, or a criminal? Clara has a right to know, hasn't she?'

'Right, rights!' Liz said. She was shaking with temper. 'The only rights you are concerned with are *yours*! It's Number One with you, first and foremost. Well, your grandfather will tell you what your rights are. He's waiting downstairs in his study.'

'I hope he'll be kinder than you are,' David said. His voice shook, as if he were fighting tears. He walked to the door, and the dog snarled as he passed; a low, grumbling snarl, upper lip lifted, his old teeth worn down but still menacing. Liz put her hand down to his collar, to hold him. 'Animals know,' she said, half to herself, half to Clara.

Clara felt very strange. As if she was outside her body and watching this scene from a long way away. She said, 'Liz, he can't be my cousin! Our mother was an only child.'

'*My* only child,' Liz corrected her. She sounded as

51

angry with Clara as she had been with David. Then her face sagged into powdery creases and she sat on the edge of the bed. The dog leaned against her and she stroked him, lifting his head and looking into his eyes as she spoke to Clara. 'Your grandfather was married before, married and divorced long before he met me. David is his grandson. His son's boy.'

Clara took this in slowly. It seemed her mind had gone rusty – as if all its cogs and wheels needed oiling. She said, wonderingly, 'Then mum has a *half brother*!'

Liz went on stroking the dog, looking down at him, her face almost hidden by the ginger wig that had slipped down a little, over her forehead. 'Not any longer. He died in a car crash. His wife was killed with him.'

Clara's mind speeded up, working overtime, everything clicking into place suddenly. Her mother's half brother would have been her half uncle. That meant David was right. He was a half cousin. Here was something else the grown-ups had kept hidden! Indignation swelled up inside her and she burst out with it. 'Mum ought to have told us. People ought to know about their relations. It was really mean of her. Why didn't she tell us?'

'Because we hadn't told *her*.' Liz sighed and pushed her wig straight. 'There was no point in it. Grandpa's first wife married an American soldier during the war and took the boy to the States with her. All those years your mother was growing up, we had no word from them. Your grandfather sent money to start with, but there was never an answer. He didn't even know that his son was dead, or that he had married and had a son of his own, until David turned up, five or six years ago. And by that time your mother had gone. Quarrelled with Grandpa and left us . . .'

She sounded very sad. She said wearily, 'You children were born and I'd never seen you, that hurt me so terribly.

52

And David made the pain worse. Calling me "Grandmother", spoiling the name for me, rubbing salt in the wound. Asking questions about you that I couldn't answer, wanting to meet you all, the three of you and your mother. His "auntie", he called her.'

Clara said cautiously, 'Why couldn't he meet us? You could have written to Mum.'

'We wanted to spare her,' Liz said.

'Spare her what?'

Liz looked shifty. She said, in a tired old woman's grumbling voice, 'Oh, just all this ancient history! Nothing to do with her, all past and gone. None of her business.'

'David's not ancient history. Mum would have been interested.'

'We thought she had enough on her plate without that great, greedy lout of a boy. Don't keep on, Clara. There are some things best left.'

'She hates him,' Clara thought, 'she really does hate him!' It scared and bewildered her, the idea of someone as old as her grandmother hating someone so much. She thought of David, coming to visit his grandparents, longing to meet the rest of his family, needing someone to belong to, now that his parents were dead. Oh, Liz was cruel to him. Heartless!

She said, 'Oh, poor David! It must be so lonely, being an orphan. We ought to be kind to him!'

She had pretended to be talking to herself, as if she were alone and thinking aloud, gazing out of the window, and was startled when Liz cackled suddenly. Not a real laugh, a dry sound. When Clara turned to look at her she saw she was smiling; a small, sly, crooked smile. She said, 'Do you think *I* haven't tried, Little Miss Charity?'

CHAPTER
7

Noel was slower to make friends than Clara and Bosie. While they bounced all over David, eager as puppies, he stood back, watching. Wary of David to start with, a bit annoyed by his boastful talk, by Sunday evening he was both puzzled and frightened.

Sunday afternoon, David and Bosie started clearing the pond, digging out weeds and mud. Or, rather, Bosie was digging. As he sloshed about, throwing spadefuls of stinking mud up on the crumbling banks, David leaned on his shovel, keeping himself clean and dry and shouting encouragement – 'That's right, Action Man' – so that Bosie, pink with pride, worked even harder, to please him.

Not to much effect, though. Most of the mud he dug up slid straight back into the pond, as Noel pointed out when he went to look. But Bosie ignored him and Clara said, 'Don't interfere, Noel! David knows what he's doing. Why do you always spoil everything?'

Liz was standing by the summer house. She was wearing a fur coat and an enormous fur hat. Beneath its wide brim her face was pinched up and sour. When Noel toiled up the path from the pond, she said, 'Had enough, have you?'

Noel shrugged his shoulders. 'They don't need me. You'd want a mechanical digger to do anything, really. And some kind of crane to lift off the dead tree. But it keeps Bosie happy.'

'Clara, too, by the look of it. She thinks David is wonderful, doesn't she?' As they walked round the summer house to the drive, Liz pouted playfully at him, putting on her bad-little-girl look. 'I'm afraid Clara's angry with me. She thinks I'm unkind to him.'

Noel wasn't sure how to answer. Liz was being embarrassing, trying to get him on her side in this childish way. But he felt protective towards her, all the same. She was the sort of person you could be irritated by and feel sorry for at the same time. He said, awkwardly, 'Clara always sticks up for people.'

Liz sighed, disappointed. She leaned on the walking stick she always used out of doors and hunched her thin shoulders, switching from little-girl to old-woman, pretending to be older and frailer than she was, to get sympathy. She said, in a fretful voice, 'I suppose *you* think he's wonderful, too!'

'No, not really,' Noel said. 'I don't really think anything. I don't know him yet, do I?'

He didn't want to admit he was jealous. A bit hurt, perhaps, by the scornful way Clara had spoken to him at the pond. But not *jealous*! Not even surprised! He was

55

used to Clara. When she decided to stick up for someone, she didn't care who she kicked in the teeth while she did it!

What did surprise him, he thought, looking at his grandmother who really did seem much older than usual just at this moment, old, small and tired under her thick, shining coat, was the way she and Grandpa had acted since David arrived. Liz had been even more lizard like, darting out of rooms when David came into them, as if she couldn't bear to breathe the same air, and sitting very still at meal times, blinking from time to time, but keeping very quiet, hardly eating. And, more surprisingly, Grandpa had been quiet, too, not complaining when David ate greedily with his mouth open, or drank with loud, slurping noises. He watched David, blue eyes oddly shy under his stiff, prawn-whisker eyebrows, and when he did speak to him, he cleared his throat first and his usually gruff voice was gentle. It was as if some strange spell had turned him overnight from a huffing and puffing old bully into a mild, elderly gentleman.

Noel said, 'I suppose Grandpa must be very fond of David.'

'Fond?' Liz said. '*Fond?* What makes you think that?'

'Well. I mean, he's his grandson.'

'Duty!' Liz said. 'He's a great one for duty, your grandfather.'

But it wasn't as simple as that as Noel discovered that evening. He was in Grandpa's study, waiting for Grandpa to come and play chess with him, setting out the board and the pretty, ivory pieces, when David came in. He went straight to Grandpa's liquor cupboard and took out a bottle of whisky. He had lifted it to his lips and was glugging down a fair swig, when Grandpa appeared in the doorway. Noel saw his lumpy cheeks darken and held his breath, waiting for the explosion. But to his astonishment Grandpa turned and shuffled away in his old carpet slippers without saying anything.

David hadn't seen him. Too busy drinking. He sat down in Grandpa's chair, holding the bottle between his knees. He was glowing and scrubbed from his shower, wearing black jeans and a black Tee shirt with a white, winged devil etched on it. Little light bulbs in the devil's eyes and at the tips of his wings flashed on and off. David showed Noel the battery he had in his pocket. He said, 'Cunning, isn't it? Want a game of chess? I warn you, I'm a bit of a champion. International class. But I daresay I could hold back, give you a chance.'

'I'm waiting for Grandpa,' Noel said, and felt himself blush. He was ashamed for his grandfather, creeping away from his own study door as if he were afraid to come in, and ashamed for himself because he had seen it. He hoped Grandpa hadn't noticed him, sitting quiet by the fire . . .

'OK,' David said. 'Another time. Right?' He lifted the bottle and took another long glug of whisky. Noel watched his adam's apple bob up and down his plump, creamy throat as he swallowed. David belched, patted his stomach and said, 'That's the medicine! That hits the spot! How about you?' He held out the bottle.

Noel said, 'I don't drink. And, besides . . .' He stopped, feeling nervous.

'Besides what?' David burped again and beamed at him blandly.

Noel tried to sound calm. 'I only meant – Grandpa doesn't like us to take things without asking. Especially not from his study. We're not even allowed to turn on the television or look at the books without his permission.'

'Scared, are you? Aw, come *on*! What can he do to you? An old guy like that.'

'I'm not scared,' Noel said coldly. 'Only polite.'

'And I'm not? Is that what you're suggesting? Just because I hit the whisky after a hard day's work?' David laughed, not very pleasantly. 'Look, let's get things on the level. This is my home. So I've a right to come and go as I please, take a drink when it suits me. More right than you, really. You've got a home and folks of your own. My mother and father are dead.'

'I'm sorry,' Noel said.

'Well, I've had to get used to it. You think a bit, though.' David gave a long, gusty sigh. 'Put yourself in my situation. How would you feel in my place? Coming over here – just a raw kid of eighteen the first time – all keyed up and eager to meet what's left of your family, and finding you aren't all that welcome! Oh, the old man's been generous, I don't deny that. Write a cheque soon as asked for it. But that's nothing to him. He's loaded, right? And I get the feeling that what he gives me is just a bribe, kind of. *Absence money* – here you are, David, now clear off, out of our sight! That's not a good feeling. It hurts me, and when I'm hurt, I get mad.'

He thrust his head forward and looked heavy and menacing. 'More so this time than usual, I think you should know that. Might as well have the cards on the table. I come here thinking, well, I might as well do a bit for the old people in return for the handouts, freshen the paint, fix the gutters or something, and what do I find? The three of you settled in, grandparents fussing around, nothing too good for you, and that really does *bug* me. I'm the oldest grandson, they should respect my position, but it's clear that you lot come first with them. I'm not even a lousy second. Just David, turning up again like a bad penny.'

'It's not our fault,' Noel said. 'We can't help being here.'

David looked at him for a moment, a long, careful look, judging and measuring.

'OK,' he said finally. 'OK. I don't blame you. I daresay we'll get along. Up to you, really. As long as you don't go tattling, behind my back, telling tales, or try pushing me out. If you do, you'll be in dead trouble, I warn you.'

Noel could only grin weakly. Though this was a silly threat – what did David think he could *do*, after all? – it seemed unkind to say so. And, 'Of course we won't push you out, David,' might sound a bit patronizing. So Noel simply smiled in a way that was meant to be reassuring, while his mind itched with questions. Why was Grandpa giving David money when he was old enough to earn his own living? If he really didn't like David, why didn't he tell him to go? And – more important, and so odd a thought that it made Noel's head buzz with excitement – how did Grandpa know that David really was his own grandson? If he had just 'turned up' as Liz had told Clara, he could be an impostor! But that was unlikely, Noel thought regretfully. It was the sort of thing that happened in books, not in real life. All the same, he tried to think of a way to find out. He said, 'You don't sound like an American, David. I mean, you haven't got much of an American accent?'

'You're an authority, are you?' David said – but wryly, not nastily. And, when Noel shook his head, 'My father never lost his British accent, and I've been in this country six years. That's quite a while, isn't it?' He looked at Noel with an expression that was hard to define. Half shy, Noel thought, half spiteful. He said, 'And when you think all that time I've been hearing about you, wondering how I could get to meet you. And my auntie, of course. But

59

apparently that wasn't allowed. Does she know I'm here now? Or is she still in the dark about me?'

He sounded so innocently eager that Noel felt mean suddenly. When his mother had telephoned on Saturday evening, he had expected Clara or Bosie to tell her, and, when they didn't, meant to tell her himself, but it seemed too big and important a thing just to blurt out. As Clara said afterwards, if their mother didn't even know she had a half brother, it was hard to know where to begin. And besides, the telephone was in the front hall and although Grandpa and Liz had been in the study with the door closed and the television on loudly, it didn't feel private.

Noel said, 'I'm afraid she doesn't know yet. I was going to tell her but she's got so much on her mind with my father in hospital, even though she says he seems a bit better, we thought – I mean, *I* thought – it was best not to worry her.'

As soon as he'd spoken, he knew that this had been the wrong thing to say. David slumped back in Grandpa's chair, his red mouth pouting and petulant. While he glared at Noel angrily, he fiddled with the battery in his pocket, flashing the devil's eyes on and off. Then he said, in a bitter voice, 'Ashamed of me, are you? Why should my being here worry your mother? I suppose I ought to have known you'd take your cue from the grandparents. You're not like your brother and sister. You're a lackey, a lick-spittle! I've been watching you, sucking up to the old fools – "Yes, Grandpa, No, Grandpa" – eye on the main chance, I'd say, from the beginning! Well, you won't get away with it, do me out of what's owed to me, with your pretty manners! I'm telling you, friend! You just keep out of my light!'

Noel was bewildered. He knew he'd been tactless, but this attack was absurd – almost comic. And yet he was scared by it. At least he was scared for a moment. Then Grandpa came in, and he stopped being frightened. Although David was a man, he'd been acting more like a stupid, bullying schoolboy, losing his temper over practically nothing, making wild, silly threats. Grandpa might be a bully, too, but he was quite sensible. When *he* lost his temper, there was always a reason, even if sometimes you had to search a bit for it. And he was old and strong, you could feel safe with him.

Grandpa was sucking an empty pipe. He said, 'Oh, there you are, David!' Just as if he had been searching for him for some time and was surprised to find him here in his study, sitting in his own, high-backed chair.

David didn't budge from it. He stayed in his slouched position and looked at his grandfather.

Noel got up from his chair and said, 'Sit here, Grandpa. If we're going to play chess, you'll get a better light from the window.'

David laughed – at Noel's 'pretty manners', presumably. He said, 'Don't worry, I'm going. I've been sweating all day, real hard labour. I could do with a rest before supper.' He heaved himself out of the chair with a grunt and took the bottle of whisky back to the cupboard. He said, grinning at Grandpa, 'Young Noel thinks I shouldn't have taken a drink without asking. House rules, it seems.'

Grandpa took the pipe out of his mouth and patted his pockets as if he were looking for his tobacco and matches. He cleared his throat and said, 'Help yourself, David.'

David glanced at Noel with triumphant amusement. 'Thank you,' he said. 'Though as a matter of fact, stocks are a bit low. If you like, I'll go down to the village tomorrow and pick up a crate or two. Might give the old Bentley an airing!'

Grandpa said nothing. But the scaly mottles on his face slowly turned purple.

David said, 'You don't mind, Grandfather? I mean, you don't drive yourself any longer. Not since the accident. Mrs Battle told me last time I was here. Knocked a boy off his bike, didn't you?'

Grandpa shambled forward and sat down in his chair. He gazed at his empty pipe and said, 'He came out of a side turning. I didn't see him.'

'Oh, I wasn't blaming you,' David said. 'Though I suppose you blame yourself, don't you? Bound to. Still, it's a shame to leave a good piece of machinery rusting away in a garage just because you've lost your nerve. I'll take care of it, you needn't worry. I'm a fine driver. And I'm not proud, either. I don't mind acting as family chauffeur.'

'What do you mean?' Grandpa jerked up his head, alert suddenly.

'I could take the kids to school, couldn't I? I know Bosie is just about bursting to have a ride in the Bentley.'

'*No*,' Grandpa said – almost shouted. Spit flew from his mouth. He took out a handkerchief, mopped his lips, and seemed to calm down. 'All right, David. I'll give you the keys of the Bentley. But only as long as you promise to take no one out in it with you.'

David smiled. 'Bosie will plague me. I would hate to disappoint the poor kid.'

'I'm afraid you will have to,' Grandpa said. 'You may use the car, David. But no joy rides for Ambrose. Those are my conditions.'

There was a long silence. David put his head on one side and considered. Grandpa was watching him anxiously. Like a couple of kids *trading off*, Noel thought, amazed. The Bentley for Bosie. Or for Bosie's safety.

'OK,' David said at last. 'That's a deal, Grandfather.'

When he had gone, Noel put the table and the chess board by his grandfather's chair and pulled up a stool. Grandpa looked at the board without seeming to see it. Then he said, in his normal, rough, growly voice, 'That young man takes after his father. Never could stand the boy. And don't you tell me that's unnatural! No manners, help yourself, rudeness!'

Which 'boy' couldn't he stand? His son, or his grandson? Noel wanted to ask, 'Why do you let David be rude to you,' but seeing the sad droop of his grandfather's face, the shake in his veined hand as he picked up a pawn, he thought it would be cruel to ask that kind of question. He was beginning to think he could answer it himself, anyway. The scene he'd just witnessed had answered it for him. David had some sort of hold over Grandpa. There was no other reason why Grandpa should put up with his rudeness. David must know something Grandpa wanted kept secret.

David was a blackmailer!

CHAPTER

8

No good telling Clara what he suspected, Noel thought. Even if he managed to convince her there was some truth in it, she would fly to David's defence, find some excuse for him.

As she did when he told her about Grandpa's whisky.

She tossed her hair back and stamped her foot like an impatient pony. 'So what? David's a *man*, not a boy! He's been here lots of times, why shouldn't he have a drink when he wants one? And Grandpa said he could help himself didn't he? That's what you told me.'

As he'd reported it, Noel thought, it did sound fairly reasonable. But what was said was one thing. *How* it was said, quite another.

He tried to explain this. 'You weren't there, Clara. David was sort of *bullying* Grandpa.'

'Tit for tat,' Clara said. 'Do Grandpa good to have someone stand up to him. He's always had things his own way. Look how he's treated poor Dad all these years! Refusing to see him because he had the fearful cheek to marry his daughter! That's *antediluvian*! Not just old-fashioned. Some kind of extinct *dinosaur*!'

'There's no evidence that dinosaurs cared who their daughters married,' Noel said. 'And I think it might have been Mum's fault as well. Just about half and half, anyway. They're both obstinate. But that's nothing to do with it, really, not with what happened with David. It was more than ordinary bullying. More as if he were threatening Grandpa.'

'I should think Grandpa could stand up for himself,' Clara said. But she sounded less certain. This was Monday afternoon and David had taken the Bentley out in the morning, sweeping off down the drive with a wild blast of the horn, and come back with a pair of pink satin roller boots with red wheels. Grandpa, coming out to examine his beautiful car to see if David had scratched it, had asked, 'Where's the whisky?' And David had held out the roller boots and said, grinning, 'I thought these would last longer.' Not like a man at all. More like a silly, impertinent boy.

Noel and Clara had been there. Noel had seen Clara frown. She was frowning now, twisting a long strand of hair in her fingers and sucking the ends of it. Trying to make her mind up. She said, doubtfully, 'It must have been dreadful for David. Both his parents dying on the same day. A car crash isn't like an illness. It must have been a terrible shock.'

'It was a long time ago,' Noel said. 'He must be used to being an orphan by now. You can't go on for the rest of your life making other people sorry because bad things have happened to you. I could say I missed Mum and Dad. I mean, I *do* miss them. But that doesn't mean I've a right to take Grandpa's car and his money and buy an expensive pair of roller boots without asking.'

He thought this was a good argument. But Clara looked at him with stern sorrow. 'Just because you think you'd have got over your parents dying, doesn't mean David has! Really, Noel, you are *rotten*! He's alone in the world and he's terribly sad about it and sensitive. And he tries so hard to be nice, even to Liz, who's so nasty. We ought to be *kind* to him.'

'You be kind, then,' Noel said. 'Leave me out of it.'

He felt lonely. Though he sometimes quarrelled with Clara, it was usually spit-and-scratch, and soon over. Now they seemed fixed on different sides he had no one to talk to. It was impossible even to imagine discussing David with Grandpa. Bosie was too young – and would take David's part, anyway. Liz hated David, which was just as bad, really. And there was no one else, was there?

He had forgotten about Mrs Battle. Soon after she arrived Tuesday morning, he and Clara were in the kitchen, washing the breakfast dishes, and she was bending over to clean out the oven. David crept in and stole up behind her, soft-footed in running shoes. He pinched her bottom and when she stood up with a shriek, put his hands over her eyes. 'Guess who?' he said, and as she turned, kissed her noisily.

She pushed him away. Although she laughed, gold fillings flashing, she sounded flustered and angry.

David swaggered and grinned. 'Same old Batty! Though you've had your hair fixed since I was here last, haven't you? Smashing colour.'

She patted her red, woolly curls. 'Oh, *you*!' she said.

66

'You and your flattery! Don't try and get round me that way. I wasn't born yesterday.'

'You could have fooled me! You look younger than ever!' He put his head on one side and said in a wheedling voice, 'Come on, old girl, aren't you pleased to see me? I'm no trouble, am I? Keep my room clean, wash my own things, appreciate your good cooking. Any odd jobs you need doing? Leaking taps, rusty ball valves . . .'

Mrs Battle said, 'If you want to do me a favour, you'll keep your big hands out of the tool box. I remember the last time you fixed the downstairs toilet. I was soaked to the skin when I flushed it.'

David slapped his fat thighs as if this was a huge joke. 'Marvellous, Batty! Caught with your pants down! I really do wish I'd seen that! I'll have to brush up on my plumbing!'

'Just leave that sort of thing to your grandfather, if you don't mind. How long are you here for?' He shrugged his shoulders and she said, flushing up suddenly, 'Don't tell me it's none of my business! Someone has to look out for those two poor old people!'

He looked innocently surprised. 'What harm can I do them, Batty? Grandmother didn't give me a hero's welcome, exactly, but I'm working on her.' He smiled coaxingly. 'Give me a chance! She'll be eating out of my hand very shortly.'

'That'll be the day.' Mrs Battle looked at him. 'No tricks,' she said. 'No tricks this time. I know you.'

Noel saw Clara's eyes darken. Well, he thought reasonably, that was a fine thing for Mrs Battle to say! Pot calling the kettle black.

Clara said, in a voice that was both icy and sweet, 'What kind of *tricks*, Mrs Battle?' And, turning to David, 'You did say you'd look at Bosie's bike for him. Check the

67

brakes before he rides it to school tomorrow. Noel tightened the front brake too much. If he puts it on suddenly, he'll go over the handle bars.'

Noel opened his mouth to protest but she gave him a cold glance and marched out, David behind her. Mrs Battle watched them go, her expression unusually serious. She said, 'If I were you, Noel, I'd look at that bike later. Unless you want your little brother to fall under a lorry.' She gave one of her loud, sudden laughs. 'Not that David means any real harm, just that things fall apart when he touches them.'

'He wants to help, though,' Noel said. He didn't like David. But he didn't like Mrs Battle much, either. On the other hand, he wanted to find out more about David. He said, 'Why doesn't Liz like him?'

'Oh, you know your grandmother.' Mrs Battle spoke as if this was sufficient answer – all the answer she was prepared to give, anyway. But then, as she turned back to cleaning the oven, getting down on her knees this time, head inside, haunches quivering as she attacked the grease with a scourer, she said, 'No point in asking *why*, not with old people. But if you ask me, he's a pest. None of my business, of course, except I get the brunt of it, don't I?'

She slammed the oven door hard, sat back on her heels and looked at Noel challengingly. 'Last time he was here, your grandmother took to her bed to keep out of his way and it was nothing but trays for me, up and down, fetch and carry, not a thought for my legs, and for all she keeps on about how she eats like a bird, she's a fussy bird, let me tell you! "Not enough salt in this soup, Mrs Battle!" Even before she had tasted it. So next time what she got in her bowl tasted like sea water. Exactly the same as I'd had, and the old boy, and David, I told her, there must be some-

68

thing wrong with her taste buds, so she drank it all down, every drop, silly creature.'

She winked at Noel as if she expected him to find this very funny. He said, 'You told us *David* played tricks!' He smiled to show he wasn't reproaching her and added, 'I know he does tease a bit.' But *tease* wasn't the right word for what had happened with Grandpa. He said, 'David took the Bentley out yesterday. I was very surprised Grandpa let him. He didn't want to, but David went on and on.'

Mrs Battle stood up, her knees creaking. 'Well, your grandfather doesn't use the car, hasn't done for a good while, not since he had a bit of an accident. No one hurt, luckily, but there was a lot of talk round the village. No business to be driving at his age, that sort of thing.'

'David said he knocked a boy off his bike, I think it upset Grandpa, being reminded.'

'Oh, David knows how to put the needle in,' Mrs Battle said. 'Nasty sly habit. If he can't get what he wants one way, he'll get it another. I know the old lady asks for it, drives *me* up the wall sometimes with her airs and fancies, but that's just between the two of us, no excuse for *him* to upset her. And of course your grandfather is caught between the pair of them, isn't he? His wife and his grandson.'

Was that all? Just that Grandpa felt he must be nice to David because Liz disliked him? There was more to it than that, Noel was sure. But Mrs Battle would only give one of her boisterous laughs if he talked about blackmail. And he didn't want to say *he* had been frightened. So he said, 'I think he scared Grandpa.'

She did laugh at that. 'That'll be the day! Scared! Your *grandfather*? I tell you what I think. You've put Master David's nose out of joint, the three of you being here, and it's made him a bit extra pushy. Cock of the walk is what he likes to be, but it's all noise and bluster. Nothing for you to worry about. A bit of an old worry guts, aren't you?'

She laughed again but in a kind way. 'Though I daresay you've had to be, with your poor daddy in hospital, but I don't like to see an old head on young shoulders. Take my advice and give yourself a rest for a bit. Things go on in the world and your fretting won't stop them. You just come to me if that David steps out of line. I've taken quite a fancy to you, with your nice, gentle ways, so you can rely on me. You can trust Batty!'

Her pale eyes shone at him, polished suddenly with such kind, warm affection, that he felt as if a weight had begun to lift from his chest. Although 'old worry guts' stung a bit, perhaps Batty was right. He hadn't been making a fuss over nothing, exactly, but 'too much imagination' was another thing grown-ups said, and perhaps he had been imagining trouble.

And when he went to look at Bosie's bike and found Grandpa already busy, spinning the wheels and checking the brake blocks, the weight lifted completely. 'Just a bit of an adjustment,' Grandpa said. 'Always keep machines in good order, that's the right ticket.'

'I was going to do that,' Noel said. 'I'm sorry.'

'Sorry? What for? My business to see Ambrose gets to school safely. Time I can't fix a boy's bike, I'll be just about ready to hand in my chips.' Spanner in hand, he gave Noel a full, cheerful smile, showing most of his strong, yellow teeth. 'You leave an old man to his job and get on with your own. Ready for school? What about Clara? As I remember your mother, girls leave everything to the last minute. Run along, there's a good lad, tell her to get cracking. On parade first thing tomorrow, bags packed, shoes polished. No last minute rush and tear in the morning.'

Clara was with David, in his room in the attic, on her knees in front of the open dolls' house. When Noel came in, she looked over her shoulder and blushed for some reason. 'Oh, Noel, isn't it lovely? Real wooden furniture, not plastic, and little gold mirrors. This room, on the middle floor, is like the big one in this house that isn't used any more. As if the doll's house was meant to be a model, not just a toy. And the dolls are so *neat*, all their clothes sewn with such tiny stitches. A mother and father, and a little girl doll, and two maids in caps and aprons down in the kitchen. And – *look* – there's a rocking horse, just like Bosie's, in one of the bedrooms.'

She smiled as she gave it to him; a sweet, coaxing smile. Trying to make friends again. But why now? He examined the little horse, beautifully carved, carefully painted, and said, 'I thought the dolls' house was locked.'

'David found the key in the desk. Just luck, he wasn't trying to find it, just looking to see if there were any old papers – photographs, that sort of thing, to do with his father.'

'Documents,' David said. 'Old school reports. Letters. His birth certificate. Every time I come I keep looking, even in places I've looked before. Hoping. You'd think grandfather would have kept something. As a reminder. You'd think he'd want to remember. My dad was his only son, after all.' He frowned. 'His son and his heir.'

He sat at the desk, a jumble of papers in front of him. Noel moved towards him and he slammed the roll top down sharply. 'Private,' he snapped. 'No need for you to poke your nose in.' But his face was so set and heavy with sadness that Noel wasn't angry. He thought of the drawer

71

where his parents kept childish things; poems Clara had written when she was very young, baby curls tied up with ribbon, one of Bosie's first shoes.

He said, 'I wasn't being nosy. But if there's nothing in that desk, I expect there is somewhere. Have you asked Grandpa?'

'He'd just slap me down,' David said. 'Your grandmother doesn't like to hear my father's name mentioned. Jealous old bitch – but she calls the tune in this house and *he* dances to it. First time I came here, he told me. "It upsets my wife to be reminded that I was married before." And you know what's behind that, don't you?' His lips curved in a sly, knowing smile. 'Money's behind it. I reckon she's afraid he'll leave something to me in his Will. That's why she tries to turn him against me.'

'I'm sure Liz wouldn't do that!' Noel looked at Clara for help. But she was sitting on her heels, apparently more interested in the little doll she was holding than in this conversation, turning it upside down, examining its pretty, frilled underclothes. So he went on, speaking fast out of embarrassment, 'They don't like to hear our father's name mentioned, either. When our mother telephones, they never ask how he is. I think they just shut off things they don't want to think about. But there's no point in asking *why*, not with old people. That's what Batty says . . .'

'*Batty!*' Clara said, '*Yuck.*' She put her hand on her chest and bent over, pretending to vomit. 'How can you even *listen* to that horrible woman?'

Noel said, 'She's not so bad. Quite nice, really.'

'Are you out of your mind? You *know* what she's like! How she treats Liz!'

Clara sounded indignant but she was blushing again. Looking guilty, too – and Noel thought he knew why. She had been gabbing to David about the jar of face cream that

Batty had hidden. Trying to cheer him up, probably, because Batty had been sharp with him, but feeling guilty now, all the same.

'Ought to put a stop to that sort of thing,' David said. 'Your poor little grandmother.'

Noel stared at him. A moment ago David had called Liz a 'jealous old bitch'. Now he was shaking his head sorrowfully, as if he were really concerned for her.

Noel said, 'It's none of our business. Batty and Liz have known each other for years. They're used to each other.'

It was clear to him suddenly. People got into habits, ways of treating each other that might seem shocking to a person looking on for the first time but weren't shocking to them. He said, 'Things go on, we can't change them.'

'Oh, can't we?' David said. He stood up, stretching his arms above his head, smiling down at them. Smiling and smiling, holding them trapped with this steady smile as if he had put a spell on them. 'Maybe you can't change anything,' he said at last. 'But I think you'll find that I can.'

He left the room, walking light on the balls of his feet, whistling merrily. They heard his whistle all the way down the stairs from the attic, across the landing, down the next flight to the hall. Then the front door opened and closed with a bang and the whistling stopped.

Noel said, 'At least he hasn't gone into the kitchen to have it out with old Batty!'

Clara put the woman doll into the drawing room of the house, bending her body to make her sit in a chair. Fiddling with the doll's skirts, spreading them out to disguise the stiff legs, she said in a muffled voice, 'What d'you think he'll do?'

'Nothing. He was just showing off. Making himself feel important.' He waited for her to turn on him, accuse him

73

of being unfair, but she only sighed. She closed the dolls'
house and left the key in the padlock. She said, soft and
low, 'I wish I'd not told him about Liz and Batty.'

'Why not?' Noel crouched down beside her. 'I wouldn't
have told him, but that's only *me*. How I'd feel.'

She sucked the ends of her hair. 'I don't know. He
looked so – so sort of *pleased*. As if I'd given him something. But it was just a look.' She glanced at Noel and said,
almost crossly, 'You weren't there to *see*. I can't explain a
look can I?'

This was more or less what Noel had said to her when
he'd told her about David and Grandpa. But she seemed
so subdued, he decided not to remind her. He said, 'I
expect you felt mean about telling him, you know what
you're like, you say things and then wish you hadn't. I
expect that was all it was, really. Even if it wasn't, even if
David *was* pleased to hear something bad about Batty,
that's not so terrible, is it?'

She shook her head. Then said slowly, 'There's another
thing. When David was looking through things in the
desk, he talked about money. And it started me thinking.
It was Grandpa's Will he was looking for, not old pictures
or school reports. I think that's *despicable*.'

Noel put his arm round her. 'Oh, come *on*. Does it
matter what he was looking for? He wants to know
something about his father when he was young. Wouldn't
you want to know, in his place? What's got into you all of a
sudden?' He shook her a little, to shake some sense into
her. 'I thought you were *sorry* for David! Alone in the
world, a poor orphan . . .'

She pushed him away and stood up. Her face was
burning. She put her hand to her burning face and said, 'I
can change my mind, can't I?'

CHAPTER
9

A kind of battle was going on inside Clara's head. She had been sorry for David. She had decided to love him. She still wanted to love him, the idea of loving him made her feel warm and happy, but other thoughts kept creeping in.

She couldn't help wishing he wasn't so fat. That was a cruel thought, really rotten and low, and she despised herself for it.

But there were other thoughts too, marching about in her mind, at war with each other. The spiteful way David had talked about Liz. On the other hand, Liz had been spiteful to *him*. It was shocking to think he might have been looking for Grandpa's Will. At least, it shocked Clara. Noel hadn't seemed to think it so awful, even though he didn't like David. Why didn't he like him? Not that it mattered. If you loved someone, what your brother thought wasn't important. But Noel was usually nice about people – so nice, sometimes, that he made her feel mean and small.

He made her feel particularly mean the next morning. They had caught the school bus at the cross-roads and as it was passing the end of their drive, David appeared on his pink satin roller boots, wearing his black Tee shirt with the flashing-eyed devil. He waved at the bus and as it gathered speed, skated behind in the slip-stream. The sort of dangerous thing a daft kid might do – but David wasn't a kid. Watching him, Clara felt her mind split, part terrified for him, part ashamed of the way he looked, the way everyone at the back of the bus must be seeing him – an overweight man in a silly Tee shirt tearing along like a crazy teenager, red-faced and grinning. When he swerved safely to the side of the road and stood on his brake wheels and someone – a blond boy – said, 'Who is that idiot?' her mind became whole again; a solid balloon of hot shame.

Shaking her head, affecting ignorance, Clara smiled at the boy, sharing his amusement at the antics of this ridiculous stranger. Then, beside her, Noel said in a cool voice, 'He's our cousin. And he was really quite safe. He's a champion skater.'

Clara turned away and looked out of the side window, sick with anger. She was furious with Noel for admitting that he knew David and furious with herself for pretending she didn't. She heard the boy say to Noel, 'Sorry. OK?' and felt sure he was staring at the back of her head, wondering why *she* hadn't answered him. He must think she was mad!

And Noel must think she had acted like Judas. When she peeped nervously at him and he winked as if to say he knew how she was feeling and wanted to comfort her, she was convinced he was only concealing his disgust out of

76

kindness, and that made her feel worse. When she felt like this, sour and lumpish and evil, she didn't want kindness! She thought of her mother who was never kind – or not in Noel's easy way. She was loving but sharp. She would say something like, 'Don't sulk, Clara. No one is perfect, we all do things we're ashamed of but if you think you've done something wrong you can't put it right by making the rest of us suffer. So pack it in, darling, take that grim look off your face.'

Clara made herself smile at Noel and then, for the rest of the journey, for the rest of the long, boring day, longed for her mother.

That evening, she was the first to answer the telephone. 'Oh, Mum,' she said, feeling relief washing through her and over her like a sweet, healing tide, 'Oh, Mummy, how are you?'

'I'm all right, how are *you*?' Faint surprise, then concern. 'Is anything wrong?'

'No. No, of course not. I just thought – I mean, how is Dad?'

'Getting on fine. They've put him on basket making. It's supposed to be soothing.'

'If he's out of bed, why can't he come to the telephone?'

'He will soon. He doesn't feel like long conversations just yet. He sends his love, though.'

'Tell him we miss him.' Clara felt her throat closing up. 'Miss you, too.'

'Poor darling. I'm sorry. Was school so awful?'

'No. Well, no more than usual, Draughty corridors, bells, all rushing about and a ghastly school lunch. Greasy sausages, junk food and chips. You know what it's like.'

'I know what you always say. I suppose all the other girls are half-witted and the teachers are morons?'

'Just about.'

Her mother laughed. Clara said, 'Our class teacher's quite nice. She asked if I was Dad's daughter. She'd seen him in that television series last year and wanted to know what he was doing now. I said he was rehearsing for an Australian tour, that's why we are staying with our grandparents.'

Her mother was silent. Clara said anxiously, 'Was that horrible of me?'

'No, my love. Dad wouldn't think it was horrible either. But you'd better tell Noel, so he has the same story. Now what else has happened? What else can you tell me?' She stopped, waiting, and then went on with a smile in her voice, teasing gently, 'Why didn't you tell me your cousin David was staying there with you?'

Clara couldn't speak. She felt as if she'd been thumped in the chest, all the breath driven out of her.

Her mother said, 'I had a letter from Grandpa this morning. Very long, rather formal.' She put on a prim, acting voice. '"If I found it ridiculous that I had never been told he had a son and a grandson from a previous marriage, I must try to accept that he had honestly believed there was no point in my knowing. He hoped it wouldn't come as too much of a shock now, but events had forced his hand."' She laughed, though without much amusement, and went on, 'And so on and so forth. I must say, I was a bit shaken. All these years, keeping this secret! Makes you wonder how many more skeletons he's got locked up in his cupboards.'

Clara said, 'That's a bit mean. You and Dad have kept secrets from us.'

'Nothing like this, I think,' her mother said. 'Neither of us has been married before, nor do you have any brothers or sisters you don't know about. And it seems that for some reason or other you and the others have chosen to keep David a secret from *me*. But never mind about that now, don't let's get into a silly argument. What's he like?'

'D'you mean David?'

'Who else? Come on, Clara! D'you think I'm not *interested*?'

'Well . . .' Clara began, and then stopped. Her heart was beating fast. What should she say? That Noel thought David was bullying Grandpa, making him hand over the keys of the Bentley and asking for money; that Liz simply hated him? Of course she mustn't tell her mother these things. She was too far away to do anything. And, besides, it was unfair to David. She said, 'I think David is very nice. I like him very much. So does Bosie . . .'

David said, from the top of the stairs, 'Thank you very much.' He cocked one leg over the banister and slid down, jumping neatly to the floor. He crossed the hall and stood close to her, smiling down, his hand stroking her hair. He whispered, 'You're a doll, Clara!'

She shook her head fretfully. How long had he been standing there listening? Had she said anything she wouldn't want him to hear? These questions, booming loud in her head, seemed to make her mother's voice very faint at the other end of the telephone. She was saying, 'That's *good*, Clara darling. Tell David I look forward to meeting him. Now I think I'd better speak to Noel and Bosie.'

Clara said, 'Yes. Goodbye, mother.' She put the receiver down and started up the stairs, shouting, 'Bosie, Noel, Mum's on the telephone, hurry!' Bosie hurtled out of his room and rushed down, pushing past her, and she went on up slowly. David was behind her. When she got to the landing his warm hand was on the back of her neck propelling her towards the next flight of stairs. He said, 'Come on up to the attic. I've got something to tell you.'

The front of the dolls' house was open. Perhaps Bosie had been here, Clara thought, and then remembered he had been to school. She said, 'You been playing dolls' houses, David?' and laughed.

She knelt in front of the house. Some of the furniture in the drawing room had fallen over, and the lady doll, the one she had settled so carefully into a chair, was upside down on the stairs.

Clara picked her up, smoothed her skirts and sat her back in the chair, speaking to her in a mock childish voice so that David would understand she was only pretending to play. 'Silly lady, don't you know you've got arthritis in your old knees, you have to be careful on stairs. What were you doing anyway? Going down to make trouble for the maids in the kitchen?'

Behind her, David gave a strange little snigger. 'She won't need to do that any longer. Old Batty's gone. I saw to that. Told you I would, didn't I?'

He sniggered again. Clara twisted round and saw that his face was red and his blue eyes excited. He said, 'Mind you, I thought a lot before I did anything. Going over what you'd been telling me, walking about all morning, worrying myself sick over the right thing to do. First I thought I'd have it out with old Batty myself, put her in her place good and proper, but then I thought, no, it's a job for the old man, he's her employer. So I went and told Grandfather what she'd been doing, tormenting the life out of Grandmother. If he didn't believe me, I said, he could ask any one of you and you'd tell him, but he saw I'd no axe to grind, no reason to lie, so as soon as your grandmother had gone to lie down after lunch he called Batty into his study.'

'What did he say to her?' Clara said. 'I mean, did he say *we* had told him?'

'I don't listen at keyholes,' David said virtuously, 'but I should think he gave it to her, hot and strong. She upped and went straightaway, leaving a filthy mess in the kitchen. I cleared it up this time but we'll all have to turn to from now on.'

He was smiling, eyes dancing at Clara. Then his smile faded. 'Why are you looking like that? Aren't you pleased? I thought you'd be glad I got rid of her.' He paused and went on in a cold, threatening voice, 'You weren't lying to me, I suppose?'

'No,' Clara said. 'It's just – I mean, what will they do? Liz said, if Batty went, they'd never get anyone else, and they're old, they need someone.'

'Aw, come on!' David had changed again; grinning now, coaxing her. 'Why should they waste money, throw it down the drain on hired help? I can shop. Bosie likes cooking, you and Noel can give a hand cleaning. As I said to Grandfather, we're all strong and willing!'

Clara said, 'We won't be here always. What did Liz say? Does she know?'

'Oh, she cried and carried on, wanted to order a taxi to take her down to the village to see Batty and make it right with her, but Grandfather put a stop to that silly notion. He told her, "What's done is done," and in the end she gave over. Said a few nasty things to me, but I've got a broad back, I can take it. Though there's a limit, of course. So far and no further, and I reckon she knows it. She went to her room and locked herself in. She'll be OK when she's thought it over, seen how the land lies.'

'What do you mean?'

'Oh, she'll learn to behave. If she doesn't, I'll teach her, won't I?'

'Poor Liz,' Clara thought, 'Oh, poor Liz!' But she didn't say it. She was too oddly alarmed and bewildered by David's pleased, grinning face to say anything. And it was all her fault, anyway, she told herself as she turned back to the dolls' house to hide the tears that were coming. Telling David about Liz and Batty was just about the most stupid thing she had ever done! Even if, in a way, it didn't matter *too* much, Batty leaving – Liz would get over it, and as David said, they could all do the cooking and cleaning – in another way, one that she was dimly beginning to see, it could be important. No one else came into the house from outside, no other grown-up, sensible person. She wasn't quite sure why this was beginning to worry her, only that somewhere in her mind, from some dark, hidden corner, she could hear a low warning note sounding, like the distant beat of a drum.

She started to put the furniture straight in the house, picking up the chairs and straightening the tiny pictures on the walls. She fitted the girl doll on to the rocking horse and picked up the two maid dolls who were lying on the floor in the kitchen. One of them was damaged, its cloth neck only hanging on by a thread. She said, 'What a shame. Though I suppose I can sew it back on. But how did it happen, David? All this *mess*?'

He was in the rocking chair rocking and rocking. He said, 'How should I know? Bosie was up here after school, and this morning Liz was poking about in the trunks in the attics, looking for some dress she wanted. The old dog was with her. Perhaps she opened the dolls' house for something or other and he shoved his head in, sniffing round. You were fiddling about with it yesterday. Perhaps he smelled you, the blind, silly old fool.'

Clara thought – 'It could have happened like that.' But the murmur in her head was louder now. A sound and a feeling. David's hand on her neck and his whisper, 'You're a doll, Clara.' She listened to the regular creak of the rocking chair as David swung it backwards and forwards and thought – 'As long as he stays in the chair I am safe!'

Then she laughed at herself for being so dramatic and silly. She said, 'Well, whatever happened, we'd better make good and sure it doesn't happen again. If Bosie wants to play with the house, he can come to me and ask my permission.'

And she locked the small padlock and put the key in her pocket.

CHAPTER
10

Bosie was in the Bentley, stroking and sniffing the leather. He loved the feel of the cushiony seats he had just finished polishing, and the rich, tangy smell. This was the third Saturday that David had driven the car out of the garage for Bosie to clean, and of all the jobs David had given him, it was the one he liked best. Washing dishes was tedious, even though Noel and Clara often helped him if they had finished their cleaning, and although he still enjoyed cooking, he was getting bored with it. The kind of meals David ordered, chops and steaks and deep fried potatoes, were easy enough to prepare, but not very interesting. And they were too rich for Liz, who pushed the food round her plate, barely touching it.

As he sat in the Bentley, waiting for David to come and inspect the work he had done, this was worrying Bosie.

Since Mrs Battle had left, Liz had eaten so little. And as he was Chief Cook, he ought to do something about it.

The only meal she always finished was breakfast. Bosie took her a tray every morning; a pot of weak tea, boiled egg and thin bread and butter. David said she ought to get up, it was bad for her not to take exercise, and perhaps he was right, Bosie thought, because she seemed very listless, staying in her room most of the time now, lying in bed with the old dog snoring almost on top of her.

He had begun to smell. The whole room stank of old dog. Some mornings, Bosie opened the window a little to freshen the air, but this Saturday morning Liz stopped him. She wouldn't even let him draw back the curtains. He had sat on the bed, watching her drink her tea and said, 'Nero smells really bad, Liz. D'you think he's ill? Perhaps it's his teeth. We had a smelly old cat once, and the vet cleaned his teeth and he didn't smell after. Shall I ask David to take him in the car to the vet? I'd take him, but I don't think he could walk as far as the village.'

'Nero isn't ill, only old like me,' Liz had said. 'If you don't like the way we smell, Bosie, you don't have to come near us. And David would only take my poor dog to the vet for one thing! "Putting to sleep" is what people say, but I call it *murder*.'

Her hand had been shaking so much she had slopped her tea over her nightdress. 'Don't mention Nero to David, please Bosie. Nor to Grandpa. It might lead to a quarrel and I don't want Grandpa to quarrel with David. Nor you, nor the others. Just be quiet and good, all of you, don't make David angry.'

She couldn't really be scared of David, Bosie thought. Or if she was, she had *made* herself scared, shutting herself up in her room for almost three weeks now, brooding because Mrs Battle had gone, blaming David. And that

85

was unfair when David had been trying so hard to see the house was kept nice, making a rota of jobs to be done and explaining that it was up to the four of them to make life easy and comfortable for Grandpa and Liz who were too old to look after themselves. It was quite difficult to do everything properly, between going to school and doing their homework, but they had done their best, and David worked too, shopping and gardening. He had abandoned the pond for the moment and was planning to plant enough vegetables to feed them all for the summer.

Even Grandpa joined in the work, although he had not been put on the rota. He was usually in the kitchen making tea when they came home from school, and this morning he was raking the gravel, bending slowly from time to time to pull up a weed. He looked rather tired and red-faced, Bosie thought, watching him lean on the heavy rake and wipe his face with his handkerchief. Just old, perhaps, but he seemed older than he had done when they first came. No more shouting or bullying; barely talking, in fact, except to say sometimes, when the children were alone in a room with him, 'You all right, are you?' with a keen, searching look at their faces.

Last night, when Bosie was doing his homework – rather late because of cooking and cleaning up supper – Grandpa had come into his room and stood beside him for a moment in silence before he said, 'All right, Bosie?' And, when Bosie nodded, he had touched his head gently with his cold, heavy hand and said, 'You're a good lad. Pulling your weight like a Trojan. Young Ambrose the Fair.'

Grandpa didn't say much to David. But he wasn't scared of him, either. If David was watching a television programme Grandpa always switched programmes when it was time for the news and David never objected. No reason why David should object, Bosie reminded himself, except that the rest of them had got into the habit of asking David's permission if there was something they wanted to see and he didn't. But that didn't mean *they* were scared of him, did it?

Liz must be going potty, Bosie decided, looking through the Bentley's windscreen at the front of the house, at her still-curtained window. He remembered that Mrs Battle had said, 'Nerves are a terrible thing,' and found himself wishing that she were still here. She would know what to do about Liz, how to coax her out of her room and her silly fears. All Bosie could think of was that she must be dreadfully hungry, and it was making her weak and frightened. Perhaps he ought to ask David to buy chicken for supper. A breast of chicken, wrapped in foil with no fat, would be good for her.

David was coming out of the door with the shopping basket, crossing the drive, stopping to speak to Grandpa on his way to the Bentley. He looked at the gravel and pointed – a weed Grandpa had missed, perhaps, because Grandpa leaned the rake against the wheelbarrow and stooped where David was pointing. David nodded approvingly and then advanced on the car. Bosie got out and held his breath while David made his inspection, examining the wheels and the shining hub caps, and then peering inside at the carpets and the upholstery. At last he said, 'That's a really fine job, man,' and Bosie let out his breath in a long, relieved sigh.

He said – feeling bold because David was pleased with him – 'Would you buy a chicken when you go shopping? A chicken for Liz. She really can't eat roast meat or fried things, they make her sick, all the grease.'

David's expression was solemn. 'I don't know, Bosie. I

do my best, trying to keep the accounts straight. It ruins the system, buying special food for one person.'

'We could all eat chicken, then,' Bosie said. 'Chicken is cheaper than beef.'

David looked at him thoughtfully. 'Even if it is, Bosie, do you think it's right that one person should dictate what everyone else has to eat? Once you start catering for fads and fancies, there'd be no end to it. Grandmother has to learn to fit in with the rest of us.'

'I like chicken,' Bosie said. 'So do Clara and Noel. It would make a change, David. And I could make a soup with the bones.'

'I don't like soup,' David said. He got into the Bentley and sat with his hands on the wheel, staring in front of him, his face still and set. Then, suddenly, his lips started twitching, a funny little smile lifting his mouth at the corners. He said, 'OK Bosie. If you feel strongly about it, I tell you what, you come shopping with me today. I'll hand over the housekeeping purse and you buy just what you want for the weekend. I won't interfere. I'll just be your chauffeur.'

He looked at Bosie with that strange, small, flickering smile, his eyes hard and bright, like blue stones. Bosie felt joy bubble inside him. 'D'you mean I can come with you? Ride in the Bentley?'

His excited voice rose, shrill and clear. Grandpa turned his head and started towards them.

David said, 'Don't see why not. Hop in. Round the other side. Quickly.'

Bosie ran. By the time Grandpa reached the car, he was climbing into the passenger seat. 'Get out at once, Ambrose,' Grandpa commanded, but Bosie couldn't obey because David had seized his arm and was holding him firmly.

'Let the child go,' Grandpa said. 'You promised me, David!'

For answer, David leaned across Bosie, pulled the door shut and started the car. Grandpa went round to the front and stood there, thumping the bonnet and shouting. Bosie could see his purple face, inflated with fury, but he couldn't hear what he said because the engine was racing. He saw David let off the hand brake, and gasped. 'David, be *careful*, you'll run Grandpa over!'

David was laughing. 'Course I won't, man. Just give the old fool a bit of a nudge, teach him a lesson.'

Bosie shut his eyes, terrified. He felt – or thought he felt – the car start to move. Then his door opened and Noel was there, tugging him, yanking him off the seat, hurting him. 'Do what you're told,' he hissed. 'Didn't you hear Grandpa tell you?'

He pushed Bosie away – pushed him so hard that he almost fell – and then turned to face David who had got out of the car, leaving the engine running, and was coming towards them.

David's face was white and solid with anger. 'Bosie, get back in the car.'

'No way,' Noel said. 'Not while I'm here. Bosie, go and help Grandpa.'

Grandpa was sitting on the ground, sideways on to the car, legs stuck out in front of him. Bosie stood behind him, hands under his arm pits, and heaved. 'Not like that, you can't lift me,' Grandpa said. He turned, got on to his knees, and struggled up, panting. 'No harm done, legs gave way, that's all.' He leaned shakily on Bosie's shoulder. 'Get my breath back, all right in a minute.'

Bosie said, 'Grandpa, look! Oh, please Grandpa, *stop them.*'

Noel was kicking David who was holding him at arm's

length and grinning. Then he let Noel go, and as Noel lost his balance, thumped him in the chest viciously. Noel went spinning away, rolling over the gravel, and got up with a long, bleeding graze down the side of his face. He went for David, head down, arms flailing. David fended him off with one hand and brought the other up hard, hitting Noel flat-handed across the eyes. Noel's head jerked back but he managed to stay on his feet this time, dancing away, out of David's reach, and then darting forward to get in a couple of punches before David gave him another blow that sent him flying again, several yards. David clenched his fists. They looked huge, Bosie saw – big and heavy as hammers. He moaned, '*Grandpa!*'

'That's enough,' Grandpa said. 'That's enough.' His voice was growing stronger. He moved towards David. He had picked up the rake.

David said, 'Keep away, old man. I have to teach this stupid brat. No one kicks me and gets away with it.'

'That's not what I meant when I said *enough*,' Grandpa said. 'Brawl if you must, though I can't see you've much to pride yourself on, fighting a boy half your weight.' But he was between the two of them now, his back to Noel, shielding him, the rake with the curved, dangerous teeth pointing at David. He said, 'What I meant was, *I've* had enough. You've stayed too long, David. Time you left now. So. Pack your bags. Be off. Do you hear me?'

David opened the car door, stretched inside and turned off the engine. It was very quiet suddenly. Quiet and still. Bosie could hear the grating noise in his chest as he breathed out, and saw them all fixed in their poses, as if in a picture. David leaning against the car with his ankles crossed and his arms folded, Grandpa holding the threatening rake, Noel behind him, blood and tears on his cheeks. Bosie wondered where Clara was. He turned to the house and saw her at Liz's window. The curtains were drawn back and Liz was beside her. Their faces were smudged and pale, staring out.

Grandpa said, 'Did you hear me, David?'

'Oh, I *heard* you, Grandfather. You want me to go.' David unfolded his arms and scratched his chest with one hand. Then he smiled broadly. 'There's one thing I don't understand, though. Who's going to make me?'

CHAPTER
11

Liz said, at supper, 'That was a good chicken dish, Bosie. So tender and such a nice, herby flavour.'

'Tarragon,' Bosie said. 'David bought some dried tarragon.'

'Thank you, David,' Liz said. 'It was good of you to take so much trouble for a fussy old woman.'

She smiled at him – actually *smiled*. She had made her face up so that she looked like a bright, withered doll, and was wearing her curled, ginger wig. She had eaten a chicken breast, a jacket potato, and a helping of spinach. Her plate was empty.

David tipped his chair back, tucked his thumbs in his waistband, and belched. 'No trouble, Grandmother. Not a lot, anyway. I just wish that Bosie had told me before about your delicate stomach. I had the funny idea that you didn't want to eat with the rest of us.'

'Oh, not at all,' Liz said. 'It was only that I wasn't feeling too well. I get these spells sometimes.'

To Bosie's astonishment, David seemed to accept this polite explanation. He said, 'Well, I'm glad that you're better. It's really nice, all of us having supper together. When I was a kid, I used to watch television and see happy families sitting round a table, laughing and talking like they do in the food ads, you know, and wish mine was like that. Instead of sitting there watching on my own always.'

Clara said, 'Were your parents out all the time, David?'

He shrugged his shoulders. 'Came home when they'd got enough drink inside them. A good steaming row and then bed, that was the set up. Not much room for me in it. Except to bash me to hell and gone if I got in the way.'

Bosie saw Grandpa looking at Noel who was still eating his chicken, taking a long time because his bruised mouth was painful. He saw Grandpa frown. So did David. He said, 'I reckon I owe you an apology, Grandfather. I'd clean forgotten you didn't want me to take Bosie out in the car. I must say I don't understand why you're so set against it. But I'm sorry, anyway.' He grinned at Bosie. 'Nothing but leg work for you, I'm afraid. Since it seems I'm not to be trusted.'

Liz said, 'It isn't that, David. Simply that the children are our responsibility and we have to take extra care. If anything were to happen we'd never forgive ourselves. But if you want company in the car, I'd be happy to come with you sometime. It's a long time since I've been on a drive round the countryside.'

Pottier and pottier, Bosie thought, gazing at her incredulously, as she beamed at David. She must have gone mad. Stark raving bonkers. No other reason he could think of why she had changed so completely, behaving in this sweet and amiable way. Particularly after what had happened this morning.

David said, 'I'll think about it, Grandmother. 'Course there won't be much time for jaunting with all the things there are to do round the place at this time. Spring coming, got to get the potatoes in, and I thought I might paint the house. A lot of the woodwork is peeling and rotten behind all that ivy.'

Grandpa cleared his throat. 'Do you aim to stay all summer, David?'

David looked at him. Grandpa held his gaze for a moment, then cleared his throat again, noisily this time, and wiped his mouth with his handkerchief.

David said, 'Just as long as you need me. Long enough, I hope, to get the place into shape, see it's all running smoothly. Like Grandmother, I feel *responsible*. I wouldn't want anything bad to happen. Not to any of you. Understand? That really would hurt me!'

Something in the way he said this, in the slow heavy tone of his voice, or in the way he looked at them, each in turn round the table, produced a strange, chilly silence. As if the air had turned colder.

Into this silence the telephone rang. 'I'll get it,' David said, springing up. He left the room with long strides, closing the door behind him.

Grandpa said, 'Well!' He looked at Liz with a baffled expression.

She said, with a little, deprecating laugh, touching her painted lips with her napkin, 'I thought it was time I took on my share of the burden. Stopped hiding my head in the sand like an ostrich.'

Clara said, 'You were marvellous, Liz. It was a lovely performance.'

Grandpa's eyebrows shot up. 'A bit overdone, wasn't it?'

Clara said, 'We have to be nice to him. It's the only way, Grandpa. He's too stupid to see we're only pretending.'

They had *all* gone mad, Bosie decided. Playing games, acting. He said, 'Why should we be nice? He was beastly to us. He hit Noel.'

Noel shook his head at him, and Clara and Liz smiled at him kindly. As if they thought he was too young to understand anything! Bosie said crossly, 'I'm going to see who it is on the telephone. It could be Mum. It's her time.'

But before he got to the door, David opened it. Bosie, running, crashed into his stomach. 'What's the hurry?' David said, fending him off, grinning down at him. 'Your mother sends her love. And your father does, too. Since I'm on my feet, I'll help you collect the plates, Bosie. What have we got for dessert?'

'Apple crumble.' Bosie looked up into David's pleased grinning face. 'Why didn't you tell us it was her, David?'

'Whatever for, Bosie? You know Grandfather doesn't like meals interrupted. And your mother was glad to have the chance of a word with me. About time we got to know each other, she said. I told her you were all fine, and she sent her love and asked me to tell you your dad was in pretty good shape now.'

Noel said, 'I would have liked to speak to my mother.' His mouth was so swollen it hurt him to talk and the words came out blurry, like a drunk person speaking.

David smiled at him. 'I thought it might bother her, hearing you sound like that. It might make her wonder if there was anything wrong. She seemed so happy. I didn't want to upset her.'

No one answered him for a moment. Then Liz said, 'That was thoughtful.'

Her voice was demure, with a crisp, mocking laugh running through it. As if she were *enjoying* herself, Bosie thought. As if it didn't matter that their mother had telephoned and David had prevented them speaking to her. He looked round the table. Noel's face was crimson between the purple and pink of his bruises, and Clara was looking at Liz with a wry little smile. Only Grandpa seemed to understand how Bosie was feeling.

He said, 'She'll ring tomorrow I expect, Ambrose. You can talk to her then. When she does . . .' He paused, his eyebrows drawn together in one long, bristly line, then went on, speaking very slowly as if he were making an important statement, 'When she does, I hope you will tell her that I am extremely glad to hear your father is better.'

This was the first time that Grandpa had mentioned their father. Bosie thought about this while he washed the dishes and tidied the kitchen and wondered if his mother would be pleased when he told her. She ought to be pleased but she might say something like, 'About time, too!' – angry because Grandpa hadn't sent a kind message before.

People were very peculiar, Bosie thought, thinking now about Liz at supper, smiling at David, asking him to take her out in the Bentley, acting so friendly when she ought to be livid for what he had done to poor Noel. And – even odder – Clara had been friendly too! That was really *disgusting*, Bosie thought, as he stumped up the stairs to his room. Clara was the sort of person who stuck up for people in trouble. She ought to stick up for her *brother*!

He flung open his door. Noel was sitting on the bed with a bowl of water beside him, bathing his face. Clara was on the rocking horse, tipping gently backwards and forwards. Bosie scowled at her, pulling one of his worst faces – his angry face, narrowing his eyes into slits and drawing back his upper lip in a snarl like a wolf.

Clara giggled. She said softly, 'Shut the door, Bosie.'

He slammed it. 'No need to whisper. They're in the study watching the telly. Grandpa and David and Liz. I mean, Liz is actually sitting there with them. What's going on?'

Clara said, 'Don't be angry. Just listen. When they started fighting, I heard Grandpa shouting, and I went into Liz's room. We watched from the window. She started to cry. She said she'd been wicked and selfish, leaving Grandpa to cope with David.'

Bosie said, 'Grandpa told him to go and he wouldn't.'

'That's it,' Noel said. 'Got it in one. Oh – my mouth *hurts*.' He held the cloth to his face and groaned. 'You explain, Clara.'

She rocked the horse, bare feet dangling. 'Grandpa can't force him to go. David's too big and strong. Liz is afraid that Grandpa will try – and his heart won't stand it, she says. He could fall down dead any minute. So we thought – we decided – the only thing we can do is be nice. If we're nice to David, Grandpa won't worry, he'll think we're all getting on fine together, and it'll make David happy. He'll feel safe if he thinks we all like him and want him to stay. Then he might get bored and go away on his own without any fuss.' She rocked a bit faster and sighed. 'That's what Liz says, anyway. Maybe she's right. I don't know.'

'I'm not going to be nice to him,' Bosie said. 'If Grandpa hadn't stopped him with the rake, he could have killed Noel. And he hates Nero. Liz says he wants Nero *dead*.' He stuck his tongue out and retched. 'It would make me *sick*, being nice.'

'You'll just have to try,' Clara said. 'Unless you want to kill *Grandpa*! I've got to try, and it's harder for me.'

'Why?'

'Never you mind.' She was blushing.

'Oh, you mean kissing and stuff,' Bosie said. 'That won't hurt you. But it won't send him away, either.' He thought, nibbling the skin at the side of his thumb nail. 'We could tell Mum.'

'*What* could we tell her? That Noel had a fight with David? That's not much, is it? And there's nothing else, really. She'd have to be here to see what was wrong. She'd have to see *David*.'

'We could ask her to come.'

Noel mumbled through his damp face cloth. 'David's always about when she rings. In the hall, on the stairs. Listening.'

'We could write a letter, then.'

'We thought of that,' Clara said. 'But it would be just as hard to explain in a letter. And she might ring up Grandpa. David's his grandson, she'd expect Grandpa to be able to sort out what was wrong. And even if she didn't ring Grandpa, even if we could make her understand what was happening, it would take her ages to get here. And if David found out she was coming to try and get rid of him, he might do something.'

'Like what?'

Clara sat almost still on the rocking horse, the tips of her toes brushing the wooden floor. She said, 'There's so much to think of. Mum being worried. And Grandpa and Liz.' Her face went white suddenly. She looked at Bosie. 'Have you ever played with the dolls' house? At any time? Try and remember.'

'I tried when I first went exploring the attics but it was locked. What's wrong with the dolls' house?' Clara didn't

98

answer. Her pale, intent look impressed Bosie. He said, 'Is there a time bomb inside it or something?'

'In a way. No, of course not. Not really. It's just that David found the key and I opened it. Then, later on, I found a doll broken. Its neck twisted off. Almost as if it was meant as a message. Some kind of threat. I mean, if David thought we were doing something behind his back, he could hurt Grandpa or Liz. Grandpa's big but he's tottery, and Liz is so little and thin. If David just touched her, she'd snap like a twig.'

Bosie felt as if his stomach was coming up into his throat. Sick and shivery. He went to sit on the bed beside Noel and crept close. Noel put his arm round him.

Noel said painfully, 'Don't frighten him, Clara. Don't be scared, Bosie. Clara's right about one thing. We've got to put up with David for Grandpa's sake because it's bad for him to get angry. But the rest is just nonsense. Even if David did break the doll, and we don't know he did, it was just a spiteful game, to scare Clara. He's a sort of blackmailer, making us all scared for each other, but that doesn't mean he would really hurt anyone. I know he hurt me, but I started it, didn't I? I kicked him first.'

He smiled at Bosie, a swollen, lop-sided smile, and held him close and tight. 'He can't do anything to us, only bully and threaten, and that's only *words*. Nothing dangerous.'

'Guns are dangerous,' Bosie said. 'And he's got a gun.'

CHAPTER

12

At first they didn't believe him. Or didn't want to believe him.

Clara said, 'Oh, Bosie, you're making things up again. Witches in the lavatory, bombs in the dolls' house. Guns! Bang-bang-you're-dead. You are a *baby*!'

She laughed and galloped the rocking horse, feet tucked up in the stirrups, hair flying.

Even Noel smiled – as much as his sore mouth would let him. 'If David had a gun he'd have told us by now. Shooting at pigeons. *Boasting!* Bound to be a crack shot!'

Bosie said coldly, 'It isn't his gun. I found it in the desk in the attic before he came here. I suppose it belongs to Grandpa. From the War. If you don't believe me, I'll go and get it.'

He got off the bed. Noel caught his arm. Clara slowed

the horse down. They both looked at him, then at each other.

Noel said, 'How did you find it?'

He told them. They listened. Their faces were so solemn now that he stopped being angry. He said, 'It's a real gun, in holster. I put it back where I found it.'

Noel said, 'Why didn't you tell us? You ought to have told us.'

'You don't tell *me* things.'

'But this was important.'

'You don't tell me *important* things.' Bosie looked hard at Clara. 'I'm just a baby.'

'Don't be pitiful, Bosie, don't act so *dumb*. You ought to know better.'

'You'd only have said I was nosy! I didn't tell you about the mice, either! I found some mice in the sofa in the big room. I was feeding them but I've been too busy lately. All these meals I've been cooking. I expect the poor mice are starving!'

'Mice!' Clara curled her mouth scornfully. 'Vermin! Who cares? People all over the world going hungry!'

Noel said, 'Stop needling him, Clara.'

Bosie's lips quivered, not because Clara was scornful, but because Noel had stuck up for him. He said, 'He may not have found the gun. It's quite hard to find. Right at the bottom of the desk under a lot of old papers. In a slidey drawer. I had to open it with my knife.'

'I expect he's got a knife,' Noel said.

Clara got off the horse, giving its red mane a thump, sending it riding free. Her eyes were excited and shining with the idea that had suddenly come to her. She said, 'Grandpa's Will! I told you that was what he was looking for, didn't I, Noel? I don't know why Grandpa doesn't just pay him off. Give him money to go.'

Noel shook his head. 'I don't think it's what he wants, really.'

'What does he want, then?'

'Oh, well . . .' Noel felt awkward. 'Someone to love him,' he thought, the words ringing clear in his mind. But they seemed sentimental. He said, a bit lamely, 'I think it's like you said once. He wants to belong somewhere. To a family.'

'Did I say that? Well, he's got a funny way of showing it, that's what I say now! Bossing us all about!' Clara slapped the horse again, so hard that its tail flew up. 'I bet you, if we had enough money to give him, he'd clear out, no question!'

'I've got some money,' Bosie said. 'I can get some more, too. I could give it all to him.'

His brother and sister turned on him. They accused him together. 'You've been stealing, Bosie!' Then Noel added, reproachfully, 'You promised mother you wouldn't.' And Clara, 'If I find you've been at my purse, you'll put it all back, every penny, or I'll tear your hair out in *lumps*. You'll be worse than bald, time I've finished.'

'But I haven't been stealing,' Bosie wailed. 'Cut my throat, hope to *die*. Why are you always so horrible to me?'

'Sorry,' Noel said. '*Sorry*, OK?'

'If he's got money, he's got it from somewhere,' Clara said. 'Running a racket at school, I expect.'

Bosie said nothing. He put his head on one side and smiled like an angel.

'Oh, leave him alone,' Noel said. 'As long as he isn't stealing, it isn't important. Money isn't important. Forget it. We've got to think what to do with the gun.'

The thought of the gun frightened him. Had David found it? No way of knowing except going to look. Did

Grandpa know it was there? If it was his gun, he must have put it in the desk, but so long ago, perhaps, that he'd forgotten about it. Although they could remind him, of course, ask him if it was loaded, that was just the sort of thing Liz had warned Clara against. Noel thought of Grandpa's old, shaking hands holding the rake. *He could drop dead any minute!*

He sighed deeply, got off the bed and went to the door. Downstairs, in the study, the television was booming. Big Ben striking the hour.

Clara said, 'It's time for the news. David doesn't watch the news.'

'He'll turn back to his programme after it's over,' Bosie said. His cheeks shone apple-red. 'I'll go and get it. He won't know, I'll be quick.'

'No,' Noel said. 'You're not to go near that desk, Bosie. Not to his room at all. Nor Clara. I'm the oldest and it's my business.' His heart was thumping, uneven and fast, but he felt strong and decisive. He said, 'When he's out of the house would be best. He's bound to go out sometime Sunday.'

David didn't go out in the morning. He lay late in bed, playing his transistor while Bosie cooked lunch and Noel and Clara cleaned the stairs and the bathrooms. When he got up at midday, he went to work in the garden. Bosie watched from the kitchen window and saw him digging up the big rose bed on the front lawn, throwing the bushes in an untidy pile on the grass. Liz, walking the lame old dog, stopped to talk to him. She was waving her hands about, as if protesting. David straightened up, laughing, and after a little he put his spade down and came back to the house with her, his arm round her shoulders.

At lunch, Bosie said artfully, 'I'm going out on my bike

this afternoon. Just for a bit of a ride. It's such a nice day. You going out, David?'

David scratched his stomach. 'I don't know. I've got a project. A lot of hard work but I ought to get on with it. If you want to plan for the future, there's no time like the present.'

Liz said, 'David is getting rid of our roses to make an asparagus bed. I was a little upset at first, but it's kind of him, really. Most thoughtful. Once the crowns have settled in, we should be cutting asparagus for the next thirty years.' She smiled at Grandpa sedately, but her eyes had a mischievous glint. 'That should take us well into our second century.'

Grandpa gave a strange, wild cry – a snorting laugh that turned into a cough. David looked at him supiciously.

Liz said, in the silky voice she always used now, speaking to David, 'You mustn't work too hard, though! All work and no play! When are we going to have the drive that you promised me? Bosie is right. It looks as if it might be a nice afternoon.'

Grandpa frowned at her severely. 'You should have your rest. Do you more good than gadding about.' Then, clearing his throat, turning to David, 'You know, young man, I've been thinking. You ought to have something more sporty than that heavy old Bentley. What about a good motor bike? I've got a couple of up-to-date catalogues. We could look through them, if you like. After lunch.'

Grandpa's face was patchily red as he offered this obvious bribe. But David's suspicious look had quite vanished. It was amazing how easily he could be fooled, Noel thought, and found, to his surprise, that he felt almost sorry.

David said, 'I don't mind, Grandpa. I mean, if you're

making the offer, I'll take your advice, you're the expert. But the catalogues can wait till the evening. I don't want to break my promise to Grandmother.' He grinned at Liz, proud and pleased. 'We'll be off,' he said. 'Soon as you're ready.'

That took some time. They had cleared away lunch and Bosie had gone off on his bike before Liz came downstairs. She wore her fur coat, and her ginger wig was anchored to her head by a silk scarf tied in a bow under her chin. David helped her into the passenger seat and fastened her seat belt. She looked expectant and happy. When David turned the car on the gravel she bowed her head and fluttered her gloved hand at Grandpa, as if she were playing at being the Queen.

Grandpa sighed. Noel said, to comfort him, 'She'll be all right. David hasn't had an accident yet. I expect he'll be extra careful.'

'Better be,' Grandpa said gruffly. He gave a sudden, coarse chuckle. 'Luckily that car is well known around here. Most people jump for the ditch when they see it. Want a game of chess, Noel?'

Noel hesitated. He was itching to get up to the attic, get the job over with. Though there was really no hurry, he told himself, fighting his panic. David would be gone for at least an hour.

He hesitated too long. Grandpa said, 'Never mind, never mind, better things to do with your time, I daresay.'

He went into his study and closed the door. Clara whispered, eyes sparkling, 'Come on, Noel. Quickly.'

'Where's the fire? Wait until Grandpa's settled down with his pipe. We don't want him coming out, catching us.'

'He never goes up to the attics.'

'There's always a first time.'

Clara heaved a deliberate, impatient sigh. 'Do you want me to do it?'

'*No*. Leave it to me. All I want you to do is keep guard.'

He went slowly up the stairs. Each step he took was like lifting a weight. He stood at the top of the first flight, on the landing, and looked down at Clara.

'It's all right,' she mouthed at him. 'Don't worry. I'll warn you.'

It wasn't really her fault that she didn't. She sat in the hall, on the oak chair beside the telephone table, opposite Grandpa's study, watching the drive through the open front door. A boring job, she thought, breathing deeply to stop herself getting drowsy. Pointless, too. Grandpa would be snoring quite soon, and David and Liz had gone for a long, pleasant drive round the countryside . . .

She was mid-yawn when she heard the car. The wheels on the gravel – and something else, too. An odd, rattling sound. She ran to the front step and saw the Bentley's smashed wing, loose and crumpled and clattering. She could see David's face through the hole he had punched in the windscreen but the rest of the glass was opaque, a mesh of silvery splinters.

She forgot about Noel. She ran to the car, hearing Grandpa shouting behind her as he came out of his study. She saw Liz trying to smile at her through the side window, wig askew, her face white. Clara tugged at the passenger door, unable to budge it; then Grandpa pushed her away, wrenched it open. He said, in a voice Clara had never heard from him before, 'Oh my love, my little love . . .'

'It wasn't David's fault,' Liz said. 'Another car at the crossroads.' She sounded quite perky, but as Grandpa helped her out of the car she was trembling. If Clara had not been there too, supporting her on her other side, she would have fallen.

David said, 'She's all right. Just a bit shaken. The other car hit us – no warning! If I hadn't wanted to get her safe home, I'd have murdered that driver! I cut my hand, too, shoving it through the windscreen. Just look!' He held out a bloody fist and said in a whining voice, 'I feel pretty shaken myself, I can tell you.'

'Never mind how you feel,' Grandpa said, 'Get your grandmother a glass of water. At the double. Come along, Clara, I'll take her weight, you just keep her steady.'

She swayed between them, teetering on her high heels. When they reached the oak chair in the hall she sat down, pushing fretfully at her wig, murmuring, 'Sorry, so silly . . .'

'Put her head down, she's going to faint,' Grandpa said. 'That's right, Clara, down to her knees, that's the ticket. Get that stupid wig off, if you can. Where's that clown with the water?'

But David had gone.

The attic windows were closed and Noel had heard nothing. He had the desk open, the papers pushed to one side. The partition beneath them was empty.

'Is this what you're looking for?' David said softly, behind him.

Noel swung round and saw the gun in his hand. David was pointing it at him. Noel wondered, for a second, why his knuckles were bleeding. Then he looked up and saw David's cold, amused smile, and the bleeding knuckles were a small part of the nightmare. The bruises on his face began to ache again, throbbing painfully.

He said, 'I was just going through these old papers.

Nothing wrong with that, is there? I mean *you* did, and they don't belong to you, either.' This sounded so reasonable, he felt a bit bolder. He said, 'Is that your gun?'

'In a manner of speaking. I've got it, haven't I?'

David's eyes were so bright, it was as if they had lamps behind them. He threw the gun in the air, caught it neatly, then aimed it at Noel again.

Noel shrank back and he laughed. 'Don't worry, it won't go off. Not by *accident*.'

'It's not loaded,' Noel said. 'It can't be!'

'D'you want to find out? No, of course you don't. A gun makes a nasty noise. You don't want to scare the old people do you? Or young Bosie, or Clara?'

Noel shook his head. David said, 'Right! We know where we stand now. I can't trust you, so I've got to lay down the rules clear and plain. No sneaking behind my back, no telling tales, no tittle-tattle to grandparents or your mummy and daddy. I'm running this show. I want us to be one fine, happy family. So if you just take it all nice and easy, that's how it will be. Nothing unpleasant will happen to anyone. Understand me?'

'Yes, David,' Noel said. No point in arguing. David was mad, he decided. Better to smile and agree. Later on, perhaps, he might think of something.

'*Yes, sir*,' David said. 'Stand up straight when I'm talking to you.'

Noel's mouth felt as if it were full of sand: dry and gritty. 'Yes, sir,' he said.

CHAPTER

13

Bosie sat cross-legged on a flat, weathered tombstone and counted his money, putting the coins into piles. It came to seven pounds and fifty pence altogether, including fifty pence he had just collected, an advance payment that didn't really belong to him until he had earned it. Not enough yet, he thought, but not bad for a start.

He liked the churchyard. It was a good place to be private. No one cut the grass round the old graves and it grew high and lush – so squelchy wet at this time of year that few people walked away from the paths, round the back of the church. There was only one person here at the moment, a woman stooping over one of the graves that were still tidy and tended, the grass cut, and fresh flowers in vases.

She wore a hat over her red, springy hair, and Bosie

didn't recognize her until she stood up and turned round. She was looking at him and he waved and called out, 'Hallo Batty,' pleased and even excited to see her. In fact, as he stuffed the coins in his pocket and scrambled hastily to his feet, a lovely feeling of comfort and safety had seized him. Batty would know what to do about David! All he had to do was to tell her how horrible everything had been since she left, how much they missed her, and she would come back and put it all right again. He was so sure she would be as happy to see him as he was to see her, that he could hardly believe it when she ignored him completely. After one brief, hostile glance, she marched past him, only a few yards away, face averted.

'Mean old thing,' he said loudly. 'Stupid fat *pig*.'

He pulled a hideous, sneering face at her vanishing back but he felt hurt and foolish.

All the way home, tears pricked his throat. When he saw Clara at the end of the drive, he flung himself off his bike and said, his chest heaving, 'I saw Mrs Battle but she wouldn't speak to me. She just walked right past me . . .'

'What did you expect?' Clara said. 'Honestly, Bosie! After the way she's been treated I'm surprised she didn't spit in your face. But never mind that, I've got something to tell you. David had an accident with Liz in the car. That's all right, I mean Liz is all right, but what happened after is more important. Noel didn't want you to know, he said it might scare you, but I said you weren't such a baby!' She drew a deep breath, filling her lungs and went on, very slowly and solemnly, 'David has got the gun. And he knows that we know that he's got it.'

She explained. Bosie listened, round-eyed. He said generously, 'Poor Clara. But it wasn't your fault.' And then, 'Will he shoot us?'

'Don't be silly. Noel says, it's only to frighten. But

we've got to be careful and do what he says because of Grandpa and Liz. I mean, they're *hostages*, sort of. We could run away, but they're stuck in the house with him, so we can't just go off and leave them.'

'They could run away, too,' Bosie said. 'We could all creep out at night, and get a taxi, and go to London, and find Mum and Dad . . .'

He stopped. Clara was rolling her eyes and sighing sarcastically. 'I can just *see* that happening! Grandpa sneaking off like a thief, away from his own house, his own grandson! I should think he'd *die* rather! He might die of shock if you even *suggested* it.' She looked at Bosie, eyes dark with anger. 'You really are stupid. I ought to have listened to Noel. He was right. You're too young to understand anything.'

She was angry because she hadn't been able to warn Noel that David was coming up to the attic, angry because she was frightened. But Bosie didn't know that. He began to weep bitterly, tears spurting from his eyes and splashing down his face, mingling with watery snot from his nose. Clara said, 'Disgusting as well as stupid. Use your handkerchief, can't you?'

He fumbled in his pocket and tugged. A handful of coins came out with the handkerchief and spilled on the ground. He knelt, still crying, and felt for them blindly. Clara jerked him to his feet. She shoved her hand in his pocket and brought out the rest of the money. She said, 'You little thief!'

She was holding him, shaking him, her face close to his. 'Stop howling,' she said, 'or I'll bash you.'

His sobs became hiccups. Through misty eyes he could see Clara grinning ferociously. 'That's better. Stiff upper lip!' she said, quoting Grandpa. 'Now tell me. Where did you get all that money? You tell me this minute.'

'Shan't,' he said, wriggling, trying to get away, but she was stronger than he was. 'You're *hurting*,' he moaned, but she only tightened her grip, pinching his arms until he gave in. 'All right, all *right*, just let go of me.'

She let him go. She picked up his bike. She said, 'Not here. Someone might come along.' She wheeled his bike into the drive and leaned it against a bush. Bosie followed her along the path to the summer house. She sat on the iron steps and looked up at him. He rubbed his sore arms and said, in a grumpy voice, 'You'll get rust on your clothes, sitting there.'

'Never mind that.' She waited a minute while he shifted from one foot to the other. She said, 'I'm sorry I hurt you. But I've got to know, Bosie. You've got to tell me the truth. However bad it is, I'll stand up for you.'

He saw that she meant this. 'It isn't *bad*, Clara. It's just – just, you might laugh!'

'I won't laugh.'

He looked slyly down, scuffing the dirt with the toe of his shoe. 'Don't know where to start.'

'At the beginning is usual.'

He said, unwillingly, 'Well, we have this Black Book at my school. The headmaster keeps it on his desk and if you get a Conduct Mark you have to go to his office and tell him and write your name in the Book. You have to write it yourself while he watches you. Don't know why.'

'He has the odd idea it might make you ashamed, I expect,' Clara said. 'And I suppose at the end of the term they add up these bad marks and put them on your report.'

'How d'you know?'

'Just a guess.'

He looked at her cautiously. She wasn't laughing but he feared she might laugh any minute. He said, with grave dignity, '*I* don't mind about it, I think it's silly to mind about Conduct Marks and Black Books, but some people do. Mostly girls. Least, it's mostly girls that give me the money.'

She was looking puzzled now. He said, 'For rubbing their names out. You write your name down in pencil. The pencil's tied on to the Book. I went to the office with a note from my teacher one day, and the headmaster wasn't there. So I put the note on the desk and I saw the Book open. The girl who sits next to me in my class, her name was written in last, and I rubbed it out. Just for fun, but when I told her she gave me twenty pence. Then she told other people.'

'I see,' Clara said. 'How much do you charge them?'

'Twenty-five pence. But I only do it if they pay in advance and if their name is at the bottom of the list. It would notice if you rubbed out higher up. Leave a space.'

'In my school,' Clara said, 'the headmaster's office is always locked up when he isn't there.' She smiled at him, the pink tip of her tongue sticking out.

'I'm not lying. Cut my throat, Clara! I don't know why he doesn't lock up. Perhaps there isn't a key.'

'Or perhaps it has never occurred to him that any of his nice little boys and girls would do such a wicked thing!' But she was laughing.

He said, 'It wasn't for me. It's for David. If he had some money, he might go away. That's what you said.'

'Blaming me, are you?'

'No. I mean, I started collecting before. Then I got the idea from you. What to do with it.'

She got up from the iron steps and hugged him. 'Oh, Bosie darling, you'd need hundreds and hundreds of pounds, I should think. So you'd better stop before you get caught. Someone's bound to find out.'

113

He muttered, 'I can't stop just yet. I've got two more names to rub out. I met these two girls today when I went to the village. They gave me fifty pence out of their Saturday money.'

'Then you'll have to give it back, won't you?'

'I can't,' he said, horrified. 'Not once I've promised.'

'Course you can, dummy. Just say it's getting too dangerous.'

She smiled at him like a kind, older sister, dismissing this childish game. She had more important things on her mind. 'We better go back to the house, or David will think that we're plotting. We musn't let David think we're against him, Noel says, just pretend everything's *fine*, and maybe it will be. If Grandpa does buy the motor bike, David might get really keen and go away on it. Noel says, he thinks that's what Grandpa is hoping. Grandpa is cunning!'

Bosie said, 'When we came, Grandpa said he was Chief. The Chief Roman. But David is the Chief now, isn't he? Like he was playing that game, "I'm the King of the Castle!"'

'Only he's playing for real,' Clara said. She hugged Bosie – to comfort herself, this time.

He said, sadly, 'Poor Grandpa.'

Grandpa was standing beside the Bentley, sucking an empty pipe. Noel, wearing thick gloves, was picking slivers of glass off the gravel and putting them into a bucket. Bosie got off his bike and looked at the smashed windscreen, the shattered wing. He said, 'I'm sorry, Grandpa.'

Grandpa nodded. 'No one hurt, that's the main thing. And no more risk of it, either. That car will be off the road for a while.' He was looking surprisingly cheerful. 'Got a good piece of news for you, Ambrose. Go on, Noel, tell him.'

Noel said, 'Mother's coming. She rang half an hour ago. She's not sure which day yet, but sometime this week.' He winked at Bosie, eyes dancing.

Bosie felt lumps coming up in his chest, in his throat. He was so happy, he thought he might burst. He laughed and went red.

'Thought that would please you,' Grandpa said. 'Though it's a long drive just for the night, as I told her. And no real need, either, everything under control here, but I expect she wanted to see for herself if we were taking good care of you.' He looked at Noel. 'You'd better get on with bathing that face of yours, Noel. Salt water will bring down the bruises.'

Bosie stared at him. Grandpa returned his stare briefly. He took his pipe out of his mouth, tapped the bowl on his palm and examined it carefully. When he spoke again there was a new note in his voice. A clear warning. He said in this warning voice, 'We don't want to worry your mother.'

CHAPTER
14

Their mother said, 'I'm ashamed of you, Noel and Clara. Apart from the fact that you've frightened Bosie – which is really quite *irresponsible*, when you should be looking after him – can't you see how unkind you have been to David? He wants to be friends with you, he actually believes that you *like* him! "We're great pals" – that's what he said to me, and he sounded so proud. How do you think he would feel if he knew you were saying these cruel, spiteful things? Even if you don't care about hurting him, and I can see that you don't, what about Grandpa? David has been such a help since the housekeeper left, and Grandpa is grateful. He'd take it hard if he knew how ungrateful *you* were, how disloyal to *him*, in a way! He thinks you've been happy, he's done his level best to look after you, not a small thing at his age, and here you are, whining behind his back because you don't happen to get on with his oldest grandson!'

'Liz doesn't like him much, either,' Noel said. 'At least, she didn't to start with.'

'Oh, *Liz*! Goodness, Noel, you ought to know her by now. Chop and change like the weather. It seemed to me that they were getting on wonderfully well, last night at supper.'

Noel didn't answer. There was no point in explaining that Liz was only pretending. Once his mother had made up her mind, there was no point in arguing with her. She was like Clara that way. He thought – 'I should have known, really!' Any intelligent person would have foreseen this! But yesterday, Wednesday afternoon, coming home with Clara from school and finding his mother in the garden with David, talking and laughing nineteen to the dozen, he hadn't guessed for a moment that she might be taken in. She had kissed them and touched Noel's face where one bruise still showed in spite of the salt water bathing and said, very sweetly and tenderly but with a smile lurking, 'I hear you had a bit of a rough and tumble with David.' As if that was all it had been, a good-tempered scrap between cousins. He couldn't put her right then, and not only because David was standing there, complacently grinning. It was so lovely to see her, Noel felt chokey with joy, almost tearful. It would have been dreadful to spoil this first happy moment. 'Later,' he'd thought. There was plenty of time.

He hadn't reckoned on Grandpa taking up so much of it. She was his daughter, of course, but from what they had seen when they came (and heard from Liz about how much they had always quarrelled) Noel hadn't expected to see them so friendly. He wasn't altogether surprised when Grandpa was jolly at supper, cracking jokes, opening a bottle of wine, making a cheerful party. 'We don't want to worry your mother,' was what he had said, and he was sticking to that. But when supper was over and they had finished their homework and David and Liz had both gone to bed, she was still in the study, talking to Grandpa.

Going downstairs, Noel had heard their voices rising and falling; his mother's quick, light, pretty laugh, and Grandpa's deep, answering chuckle. When Noel had opened the door, Grandpa was leaning back comfortably, legs stretched out, ankles crossed, smoking his pipe, and his mother was sitting on the floor by his chair, one arm on his knee. She had smiled at Noel without moving and said, 'Goodnight, darling. You don't mind if I don't come up, do you? It's such a long time since I had a really good talk with my father.'

She had looked so contented, curled up on the floor, that Noel had felt tender towards her. 'That's all right,' he had said. 'We're all right. Talk to Grandpa. Sleep well.'

But sometime in the night, Bosie had crawled into her bed frightened and weeping after a nightmare. And in the morning she had woken Clara and Noel with a cold, angry face.

She was so angry, she gave them no chance. Not that Clara would try. Unfairly attacked, she closed up, stolid and sullen, eyes black with her rage.

Noel did his best. 'You haven't told us *exactly* what Bosie told you. That's not fair. If you don't tell us, we can't explain, can we?'

She looked at him with a grim little smile. 'It'll take some explaining. He didn't want to go to school, was what he said first, and I thought he must be in some kind of trouble. Then it came out. He didn't want to go to school in case David shot Grandpa and Liz. Clara had told him, it seems, that David was holding them hostage. At gun point, apparently. Poor little Bosie! He thought he ought to stay home and protect them.' She sniffed with outrage. 'What a story to tell him!'

Noel said, 'It isn't quite like that. But David does push us around. Even Grandpa. And he's got Grandpa's gun.'

'Do you really imagine that your grandfather is the sort of man to keep a loaded gun in his house? Really, you are behaving like children.'

'We are children,' Noel said.

'Don't quibble. You know what I mean. It was childish to make up silly tales and scare Bosie.' But when she spoke again she was gentler. 'I know David is odd in some ways. Young for his age, overanxious to please. But his heart's in the right place. And you ought to make some allowances for him. How would you feel if you had no mother or father, no brother or sister. I'm particularly surprised at you, Clara. It's not like you to be so cold and uncaring.'

Clara lifted her gaze to the ceiling and sighed. Her mother said, 'I thought that you liked him. You told me you did, on the telephone.' She waited for Clara to answer, then shrugged her shoulders. 'All right, sulk if you want to!'

Downstairs, Bosie banged the brass gong for breakfast. She said, 'Listen, darlings, there isn't much time now. Just one or two things. I can see you don't like David. I don't blame you for that, only for upsetting Bosie. I thought he was quiet last night while we were having our supper. At least I know why now, that's something. And I hope for the rest of the time that you're here you'll try and be sensible. There's always trouble in families, but people fight and make up. Look at Grandpa and me!' She smiled suddenly. 'David's part of his family, too. He feels

119

responsible for him. If there was anything wrong, he'd have told me.'

Clara said, in a rough voice, 'No, he wouldn't. He wouldn't want you to know he wasn't still King of the Castle.'

Her mother laughed. 'I daresay Grandpa has had to make quite a few small adjustments just lately. First time in his life he's had to look after three children for one thing. Have you thought what a difference that must have made to him? But he hasn't complained to me, bless him!' She went to Clara and kissed her. 'I'm glad you found your tongue at last, darling.'

She was leaving. Bosie had gone already, ridden off early to school on his bike. She had kissed him goodbye, kissed her mother and father. On her way to the car with Noel and Clara she stopped beside the asparagus bed where David was working. The trench was eight foot long and nearly six foot down now, and he was deep in it.

She said, 'What a tremendous task, David!'

He laughed up at her, the sun in his eyes. 'You have to dig deep for asparagus, Auntie. Can't disturb the crowns once they're settled in, so you have to do the work properly. Some of this earth will go back, but you have to mix in a load of manure if you want a good crop. I expect Noel will help me.'

Noel said, 'Yes, of course, David.'

She glanced at him quickly, frowning a little, as if something about his listless tone troubled her. Then Grandpa, taking Nero back to the house after his morning walk, called out, 'Watch your time, Noel. Don't want to miss the school bus,' and she turned to wave at him.

'Goodbye, darling Pa!' She watched him, her face happy and glowing, as Nero faltered at the steps between the stone lions and Grandpa bent to lift his hind quarters before he waved back to her.

She said, 'He's got very lame, hasn't he. Poor Nero.'

'Blind and smelly too,' David said. 'Ought to be shot, that old dog.'

'Well, it comes to us all,' she said, smiling regretfully, meaning no more than that Nero was old and would probably die soon. But to Noel and Clara, standing silent beside her, the asparagus bed that David was digging took on the shape of a grave.

CHAPTER
15

The headmaster's office was locked. It had been locked all the week. Monday, Tuesday, Wednesday. Just chance, Bosie had told himself to begin with. But each day he had grown a little less hopeful and this Thursday lunch time, slipping out from the dining room while everyone else was still eating, he knew it was no use even before he tried the handle. He said several rude words under his breath, gave the locked door a kick to relieve his feelings, and walked away down the empty corridor, shoulders hunched, whistling bravely.

By the time he found the two girls in the playground he was indignant. 'He must have got some money stashed away in that office. Or private papers, or something. Though I think it's pretty stinking mean, really. As if he doesn't trust people. Locking things up as if we were all thieves and robbers!'

The girls giggled. A stout girl with thick legs and warts on her stumpy fingers, and a small, sweet-faced, dainty blonde. Funny how girls always seemed to pair off like that, Bosie thought. Fat-and-Plain, Thin-and-Pretty.

'Not thieves,' Fat-and-Plain said. 'Just people who rub names out of Black Books. He was bound to find out sometime. Just our lousy luck.' She only pretended to groan. She was always in trouble. One more Black Mark hardly mattered.

'Never mind, Bosie,' the pretty girl said. 'You can't get through a locked door.'

'Window's open, though,' Bosie said, squinting up at it and lowering his voice because the headmaster was there, back from lunch, looking out at the playground. The window was too high to reach from the ground but there was a ladder kept in the bike shed. He didn't tell the girls this – he didn't want them to think it could be so easy. 'I'll fix it somehow,' he said, sticking his hands deep into his pockets and swaggering boldly. 'Just leave it to me.'

They were nice girls. If they had been nasty he might have given them their money back, told them to go jump in the river. But because they were nice he was put on his mettle. All the same he might not have done it, gone back later that day, in the dark, after tea, if he hadn't been feeling so miserable.

It wasn't only his mother coming and going like that. Although last night when she'd cuddled and comforted him he was sure that now he'd explained about David she would stay and look after them, he hadn't been too surprised when she left in the morning. Grown-ups seldom understood what you told them. It was like playing

123

Chinese Whispers, he thought. You said something to them and they turned it round in their head to mean something different.

What made him more miserable was the way Noel and Clara treated him when he came home from school. They weren't unkind – in fact, they were extra nice to him. Noel gave him a bar of nut chocolate and helped him peel the vegetables for the casserole they were having that evening, and Clara said that if he felt scared in the night he could sleep in her bed if he wanted. But then they went off together to Clara's room, and when he went up to ask if he could borrow Noel's torch, they stopped talking the moment he opened the door, and started again as soon as he closed it.

Whispering. Leaving him out. 'Don't let's tell Bosie!' Secret smiles and sly looks. Oh, he ought to be used to it, he thought, feeling tearful and savage, lugging the heavy ladder out of the bike shed. It took all his strength to carry it the small distance to the place he had marked out in the daylight, a bit to the right of the office window, between the sill and a drain pipe. If he kicked the ladder sideways, climbing on to the sill, the drain pipe would hold it. Although it was dark, he could see the white paint of the window, and tested the ladder's position by shifting it slightly until he heard the faint *clang* from the pipe.

By this time he had more or less stopped being miserable. Still a bit angry with his brother and sister, but there wasn't much room for that, either. He was too scared and excited – quite a good mixture of feelings. Hands a bit sweaty, but head nice and clear. He climbed carefully, testing each rung. The ladder had been lying in the bike shed among last year's damp leaves and might well be rotten. He could break a leg. Or – he was halfway up when this struck him – the window could be closed when he got there. Closed and latched. Part of his mind hoped that it would be.

But it was open. Not very wide, and he couldn't push the lower sash up any further – it was either too stiff, or held by some kind of bolt – but wide enough for a thin boy. He dropped Noel's torch into the room and eased himself on to the sill. His head and shoulders went through the gap with a bit of an effort. Lying on his belly, he felt the ladder shift before his toes left it, but there was no sound from the drain pipe so it could only have moved very slightly. Everything was going very well so far. He had even remembered to turn his belt round so that the buckle wouldn't catch on the sill as he slithered over it, toppling neatly on to his hands and walking them forward until he was able to draw his feet after him.

He felt for the torch and crouched under the window to get his breath back. Looking out, he could see the bare trees of the churchyard; twiggy branches black against the yellow light of a street lamp beyond them. The school had once been part of the church but new classrooms and offices had been added at different times and only the caretaker lived in the old School House now. There was a blue flicker from one of his windows. Bosie hoped there was something good on the telly to hold his attention. There was no blind to pull down in the office, no curtains.

Cupping his hand over the torch beam, Bosie tip-toed across the room. On the headmaster's desk, the Black Book lay open with its thick pencil dangling on a length of string. Bosie got out his rubber and tucked the torch under his arm to leave his hands free. Then he saw that the most recent names on the page had been written in ink.

He was stunned – and then furious. 'What a cheat,' he thought, 'what a mean, sneaky trick!' He hadn't got an ink rubber. Even if he'd had one, ink rubbers left an obvious mark. Clara had some white stuff called Liquid Paper that she used when she had made a mistake, to blot out the wrong word, but there was nothing like that on the desk. Just a big diary, a tray of ball points and fountain pens. And a bottle of ink.

He clicked his tongue – *Tchk, tchk*. It helped him to think. If he couldn't rub the names out, he could make them unreadable. He opened the ink bottle and tried to trickle the ink over the names that came last on the list, not bothering to check if they were the ones he'd been paid for, but the torch slipped under his arm, hitting his hand holding the bottle, and rather more than a trickle came out.

Ink on the desk, dribbling fast over the edge. Struggling for his handkerchief, tucked too tight in his pocket, he dropped the bottle and it landed upside down on the carpet. For a small bottle, it seemed to hold an enormous amount. Gallons and *gallons*, he thought, as he knelt and mopped at the black, spreading stain. Ink everywhere, on the Black Book, the desk and the floor; on his fingers, on his handkerchief, on his jeans. Unthinking, despairing, he wiped his inky hands on his sweater, breath coming in sharp, painful sobs.

He made himself stop. No good crying! It was done now. No doubt the headmaster had guessed what was going on, or he wouldn't have locked up the office, seen that the names were written in ink instead of in pencil. But guessing was one thing, knowing another! Now he would know *exactly* what one of his students was up to! And that, Bosie realized, with sudden, heart-stopping panic, was something much worse than rubbing out names in the Black Book. It was Breaking and Entering. Up the ladder and in through the window. Like a real burglar . . .

He saw what to do. No need to take anything. Just make

a bit of a mess as if someone, some grown-up intruder, had been searching the office for something. And, blundering about, had spilled ink over the Black Book by accident.

Being naturally tidy, he hadn't much taste for it. He opened a couple of drawers, emptied a waste paper basket, scattered a few files on the floor. He forgot about the ink on his hands until he'd spread it about, every file that he'd touched, each drawer handle. Well, it couldn't be helped. If they suspected an outside job, a real burglar, they wouldn't bother to go round the school taking finger prints. He had to trust to that, anyway.

What would a burglar look for? Bosie opened a cup-board. The door stuck at first and then flew open, almost knocking him over, a hard, heavy shower of tumbling text books hitting his knees and his ankles. Elementary Physics, Junior Biology, First Steps in French. Not much there for a hard-bitten villain! He shone the torch on the shelves and found a more likely attraction, a padlocked tin box with something that rattled inside. Keys or money. Mustn't take it away because that would be stealing, just pretend that someone had attempted to find out what was in it. He wrenched at the padlock, trying to force it, and then, in a burst of frustration threw it away from him. It bounced off the wall and crashed to the floor, making so much noise that afterwards the silence seemed loud – a kind of thick boom in his head. The booming silence made him weak at the knees. He rubbed his inky, sweating hands on his jeans and found his legs shaking.

He switched the torch off and walked on these shaky legs to the window. The ladder was still there, going down into darkness, so were the yellow street lamp and the trees in the churchyard, stirring now in a little wind. Although he registered that something was different about the view from the window, his mind was too tired and smudgy to sort out what it was. He wriggled over the sill, feet first, wondering vaguely if he should try again to push the sash further up to make it look as if a grown man could have squeezed under it, but he hadn't the energy.

He felt so weary, all his bones aching, that even when he remembered what it was that was missing, the blue telly flicker from that other window, he didn't worry about it. Perhaps the caretaker had gone to bed, he thought, yawning and sleepy, ready for bed himself as he climbed down the ladder.

They let him get safely down before they turned on the car headlights and started shouting.

CHAPTER
16

'Where's Bosie?' David said. 'Time's getting on. Supper ought to be ready. I'm hungry.'

He stood in the doorway of Grandpa's study, his red and gold crash helmet under his arm. He wore a black leather cat suit and knee-high leather boots. All that new gear as well as the big Triumph bike! He ought to be grateful, Noel thought. Not greedy and petulant. He said, 'The casserole's in the oven and the table's laid. Bosie's out.'

'In the dark?'

'He borrowed my torch. And he's got lights on his bike.'

'No business to be out after dark at his age,' David said. 'And I didn't give him permission to be late for supper.'

Silence. Grandpa stared into the fire and Liz bent over the game of Scrabble she and Clara were playing. In the silence, Noel could hear Clara grinding her teeth. 'Humour him,' they'd decided, 'let him play King of the Castle,' but it went against the grain of her nature.

David said, 'Right. I'll show Master Bosie. No supper for him when he comes home. Seven o'clock sharp, we'll start without him.'

Still no one spoke. No one even looked at him. Only Nero, lying on the hearth, lifted his head and snarled softly. Got more guts than the rest of us, Noel thought, ashamed.

He said, 'That's for Grandpa to say.'

'OK,' David said. 'Let him say it.' He closed the study door. They heard his heavy boots on the stairs.

Grandpa said, 'Hmph. I suppose Ambrose knows the time. Do you know where he went?'

'He often goes off by himself,' Clara said. 'But he's usually back before now. Perhaps his watch has stopped.'

Liz looked anxious. 'I hope he's all right.'

'Bound to be,' Grandpa said heartily. 'Independent little chap. Probably gone to see another lad in the village. Don't start fretting.'

But he looked at the clock on the mantelpiece. Of course he was worried, Noel thought. Just not willing to show it. He was playing the same game as the rest of them. *Don't upset David.* Liz was thinking of Grandpa's frail heart. And Grandpa was trying to keep the peace, for his wife, for his grandchildren. David had turned them all into cowards, protecting each other.

Noel said, 'Bosie really is late. We can't just do nothing. I'm going to ask David to go out on his bike and start looking.'

He left the study before they could stop him. As he ran up the stairs, he saw light streaming out from the big, unused drawing room. He went through the open door and saw David admiring his reflection in one of the heavy gilt mirrors. Still in his leathers, booted feet wide apart, head thrown back, the gun in his hand. He saw Noel in the glass and swung round to face him, resting the muzzle on his bent forearm, pretending to aim it.

Noel felt a hollow pain in his stomach, ice down his spine. Then he saw David's expression, teasing and foolish.

He said, 'Please don't point that thing at me. I don't like it.'

David lowered the gun. He said, amiably, 'Sorry. Frightened you, did I?' He looked round him and gave a deep, satisfied sigh. 'This really is a fine room! Really gracious. D'you know what I'd like to do? Fix it up, clean the chandeliers, make them sparkle, take those ratty old covers off all the furniture, get the piano tuned. I bet Grandmother can play. We could come here in the evenings and have a really good time, all of us. Better than watching the telly. A bit of singing and dancing.'

His plump, babyish face was dreamy and flushed. 'Like people in films. You know? Elegant. Your mother would like that. She's an elegant lady. I bet she's got some nice floaty dresses. It would be a surprise for her when she comes visiting next. I really would like to have a good surprise for your mother.'

He smiled at Noel, his plump, red mouth curving sweetly. 'I really fell for her, do you know that? I thought, if she saw this room, all gleaming and polished, she might decide to settle down with us.'

Noel said, uncomfortably, 'I don't think – I mean, of course we could clean the room up. I expect Liz would let us. Though there isn't much point. The study's much cosier, just for two people. Once we've gone . . .'

David said, 'But you're not going, are you?'

131

His surprise seemed quite genuine, his expression puzzled and innocent. As if he were so caught up in his dream, in the Happy Families game *he* was playing, that he really believed they would all live here with him for ever and ever.

Understanding this, Noel was more frightened suddenly than he had been by the gun. Or frightened in a different way. Fear that was mixed up with something else, a strange kind of sorrow. If only life could be like that! Everything as you wanted it, kindly and pleasant, everyone always happy together, smiling and singing and dancing.

He stammered, distracted, 'I don't – I mean, I don't know . . .' And then heard a sound outside. He said, with relief, 'Someone's coming!'

He went to the window and opened the shutters. A car was stopping outside the front door. No siren, but the blue light on the top was turning and winking.

He said, 'It's a police car!'

David was beside him. He said, in a strange, choked voice, 'So that's it. That's it, is it? I never thought. How *could* they do that to me?'

Noel only half heard him. He was pressing his face against the glass, peering down, watching the driver get out of his seat and open the door for his passengers. All Noel could see – for ages, it seemed – was his bent, uniformed back. Then a policewoman got out. And a small figure, a white face, looking up. A piebald face, rather – pale skin covered in curious splodges.

'Bosie!' Noel said. 'What's happened to Bosie?'

But David was no longer there. Noel said, to the empty room, 'It's Bosie come back.'

And rushed out, down the stairs.

CHAPTER
17

The police had gone. Bosie sat on Liz's lap, head on her bony shoulder, sucking his thumb. His lashes lay curled on his inky cheeks, hiding his eyes. He looked quite exhausted.

Grandpa was in the hall, talking on the telephone to the headmaster. They could hear the occasional word through the closed study door. *Disgraceful. Apologies. Prank.* Bosie didn't seem to be listening, but when Grandpa laughed, Noel saw his eyelashes flutter. 'Foxing,' Noel thought. Foxy Bosie! Poor little fellow! Trust him to know how to get out of trouble!

As it seemed he had done. Grandpa came into the study, rubbing his hands, red spots burning his cheekbones and forehead. He was doing his best to conceal his amusement. He said, 'Well, that's it, Ambrose. Off the hook. The headmaster is making no criminal charges. Decent of him, I consider. I suppose he thinks you've had a bad enough time of it, police picking you up, giving you a good talking to down at the station. But you're to be punished, mind! That's how he expects you to look at it. Suspended from school for the rest of the term. Can't have you back, he says. A bad example. What he means is, your classmates might treat you like some sort of hero. Can't have that, naturally. Bad for discipline.'

He started to chuckle, then went in for a long, throat-clearing session and blew his nose like a trumpet. He sat down, hands on knees. 'Not that I approve, mind. Too much softness around nowadays. In my young day you wouldn't have got off so lightly. A good thrashing, at least.'

'Don't be unkind, dear,' Liz said. 'You know you don't mean it. And the child is so tired.'

Bosie said faintly, eyes still firmly closed, 'I thought they were going to lock me up in a dungeon. But they were quite nice. They gave me a cup of tea. I made myself drink it because they meant to be kind, but they put sugar and milk in it, and I only really like weak tea with lemon.'

'How thoughtless of them not to inquire,' Grandpa said. 'What an ordeal!' Then, as sternly as he could manage, 'You did a very wrong thing, young man. I hope you're ashamed.'

Bosie opened his eyes. 'I said I was sorry. I promised I would pay for the damage.'

'So I should hope,' Grandpa said. 'I told the headmaster I would send a cheque, but you will pay me back, every penny!'

'It won't cost very much,' Bosie said. 'It was only a bit of ink. Ink washes out.'

'Hmph,' Grandpa said. 'It will wash off you, too, I hope. Get along, quick sharp now, up to the bathroom. Wash in the water and not on the towels and change your clothes while you're at it. Clara, you'd better get the food on the table. Let's hope it's still edible. Noel, you had better call David. Can't think why he's not down already. Shouting for supper. I thought he was hungry.'

'He's gone,' Noel said.

They all looked at him. Grandpa and Liz and Clara. And Bosie, wide awake now he knew nothing dreadful was going to happen, slid off Liz's lap and stood staring.

A long time passed – at least, it seemed a long time to Noel – before Grandpa said, 'How d'you mean? *Gone*. Come on, out with it!'

'What I said. He's left. Taken his things. I – I heard the bike start up while the police were here, talking, and I went to the attic to look. I think the police frightened him.'

He stopped. They all looked so disbelieving. And, somehow, accusing. But perhaps that was just in Noel's mind. He said, 'I ought to have stopped him. But I didn't know, did I?'

'Didn't know what?' Grandpa said. 'No reason why he should be afraid of the police, not to my knowledge.'

'There was the accident,' Liz said. 'But it wasn't his fault.'

Noel said miserably, 'It wasn't that. He did tell me, but I didn't listen properly. I was thinking of Bosie. He thought the police had come to get rid of him. That we – that *you'd* called them. Either Grandpa or Liz.'

He didn't understand why he felt so ashamed and so guilty until Liz explained it. She started to cry. 'The poor fool. So unhappy, so lonely . . .' Round, glittering tears rolled down the grooves of her face like small jewels.

135

Clara knelt beside her, trying to comfort her. 'He was a *menace*, Liz. Really! You hated him!'

Liz nodded. 'I know, dear,' she mourned. 'That's why I'm so sorry.'

CHAPTER
18

Clara was astonished to find that she was the only one who was really glad David had gone. Liz and Noel had disliked him so much to begin with. Now they were sorry for him. And Bosie seemed simply indifferent. He said once, 'Course, it was me got him to go in the end, bringing the police car,' but when Noel told him that was nothing to be proud of in the circumstances, he shut up and didn't mention David again. He was like that, Clara thought, when he'd had a bad dream. Once it was over and he was no longer frightened, he forgot all about it.

Grandpa kept his own counsel. The next Saturday morning, watching Noel and Clara fill in the trench David had dug, so that Liz could plant some new roses, he said suddenly, speaking more to himself than to them, 'At least he's got the bike.' And then, with a kind of gruff sadness, 'A bike can be a good friend.'

Clara heard Noel sigh and knew what he was thinking. Poor David. The Lone Rider. The Traveller with no place to go. Then she thought – how disgustingly *creepy*! Easy to pity him now he wasn't here, scaring them witless! Why were they all so sure he wouldn't come back? She heaved at a huge spadeful of earth, spattering Grandpa's shoes with it, and said, 'All I hope is he gets nice and far away, like five hundred miles, before he smashes it up.'

Grandpa didn't reproach her as she expected. He said, 'He won't come back, Clara. Gone for good.' He sounded quite certain of this, but not feeling it very much one way or the other. He looked at her for a bit, scratching the bristles at the side of his mouth with the stem of his pipe. He said, 'You've done enough digging. Let Noel finish it. Much too hard for a girl.'

'I'm stronger than Noel,' she objected. But Grandpa had been kind, understanding how she felt about David, and she wanted to please him. She did her best to smile in the pretty, agreeable way she supposed Grandpa thought a girl ought to smile, and walked to the house with him.

He said, 'Once you've cleaned up, I daresay Liz and Bosie could do with some help on the catering front. Special dinner tonight. Celebration!'

He was grinning. She thought – 'Farewell to the unwelcome guest!' She was afraid Grandpa would be upset if she came out with that, so she said diplomatically, 'It's nice when things get back to normal.'

'I hope that you'll think so.'

'Oh, I already *do*,' she said, smiling more naturally now, thinking how much better he looked since David's departure; standing straighter, walking better. Not a shuffling,

138

apologetic old man any longer! She took his big, cold hand and squeezed it.

'Good,' he said. 'Very good.' He sounded puzzled, she thought. As if she had given him the wrong answer. Or one that didn't quite fit, anyway. He was looking down at her, jerking his pipe in his mouth, his mottled face darkening. He said abruptly, surprising her, 'You must miss your father.'

She nodded – a little cautiously, but since there seemed nothing in his expression to suggest anything other than a kindly interest, she said. 'Dad always listens, that's the big thing. Not the *main* thing, of course, but important. Mum listens too, but she doesn't listen so well.' She thought that her father would have understood about David and smiled to herself as she saw a good way to get her own back on her mother. 'Mum is like some kind of wild, express *train*! Once she's got set on a track she goes thundering on. You'd have to throw bombs if you wanted to stop her. Or hurl yourself on the line, shouting and screaming.'

Grandpa chuckled and snorted, so ready it seemed to share this joke with her, that she completely forgot he had tried to stop her mother getting married; that he probably still hated her father. She said, 'Dad always knows how people are feeling, and usually what they are thinking. Mum says he's sensitive, that's what makes him such a good actor, but it really goes back to listening. He watches your face while you talk and he doesn't make up his mind until you have finished. You can tell him all you want to, without holding back the bad bits, and he never gets angry.'

They had reached the front steps. Grandpa wiped the earth off his shoes on the iron foot scraper, taking rather a long time about it. He said, without looking at Clara, 'When you do see him, it might be as well to hold back a little. A few bits here and there. Ambrose and his silly nonsense. And, well, other troubles. A man who's been sick doesn't want to be bothered.' He looked at her then, very straight. 'You understand me, I hope? Good girl! No lies now – no need for that. But as you said, back to normal. So no point in raking over the ashes. Keep things in proportion, that's the right ticket!'

She knew then. Or half knew. She put it aside. She said nothing to Noel or to Bosie. As long as she kept it secret there was a chance it was true. But it was too much to hope for. She was afraid to believe it.

Even when Liz announced, with a pleased, playful smile, that she was going to lay the table herself, no one need help her, she didn't dare peek into the dining room to see if there were two extra places. Even when she heard the car . . .

She stood in the hall, feeling dizzy and sick. Liz came down the stairs in a long, purple dress, embroidered with sequin butterflies. She said, 'Why don't you go and see who it is, Clara? Have you lost the use of your legs?' Behind Liz, Noel and Bosie hung over the banisters. Noel turned white. Bosie flushed crimson.

Clara felt her own cheeks grow hot. She wanted to run and hide. But she opened the door.

Her mother was getting out of the car. And her father. He was paler than she remembered, and thinner; his shabby overcoat hung baggily on him. He was smiling and holding his arms out.

He hugged them all, kissed them all. And then came up the steps between the stone lions, one arm still round Clara.

Grandpa was waiting. He said, 'Ah! Here we are, then!' in a deep, challenging voice that locked Clara's breath tight in her chest. She knew his threatening manner meant nothing, that it was Grandpa's habit to growl when he met someone for the first time, but her father didn't know that. Suppose Grandpa said something hurtful as he had done when they came, calling them 'The little children of the poor', and making their mother so angry! She looked hard at Grandpa, ready to fly at him, but all he said was, 'About time, if you want my opinion. Glad to have another man in the house.'

Clara let out her breath in relief and her father said, 'Thank you, sir. I'm glad to be here,' smiling at Grandpa, and then, beyond him, at Liz. He said, 'What an unusual and beautiful dress,' which was just the right thing to say. Liz blinked shyly and happily and Clara knew all was well.

They had beef for supper cooked in a crisp pastry case and mashed potatoes with grated onion and parsley and a lemon meringue pie. 'Ambrose is a remarkable cook,' Grandpa said when the pie was served. 'Even managed to teach me a thing or two. How to boil an egg! Quite an achievement!'

He gave a rumbling laugh like a low roll of thunder and little smiles and chuckles ran round the table like echoes. 'Mind you,' Grandpa said, 'I hope he branches out when he's older. Good food is a fine thing, but we eat to live, not live to eat. All right for a boy to be keen on his stomach but a grown man shouldn't be greedy.'

Clara saw his sly, dancing look, and knew he was testing her father. What did Dad really think was a man's occupation? But she wasn't worried now. Although he was so polite and gentle, her father was a good match for Grandpa. He said, in his lovely, rich, actor's voice, with a hint of respectful amusement, 'I think that if Bosie decided to be a chef when he was older, that wouldn't mean he was greedy. Just that he had decided to exercise one of his talents. But he has plenty of others. He's a great organizer, good at planning and fixing. It's early to say, but I think he might enjoy running some kind of business. He likes making money.'

'Does he now?' Grandpa said. He peered under his eyebrows at Bosie, then went on hastily, 'Of course we've been grateful for his excellent cooking, no doubt about it. We've been through a sticky patch since the housekeeper left. But they've all pulled their weight, you'll be glad to know. Not just Ambrose, but Noel too, and Clara.'

'And David,' Noel said. He had made up his mind to be fair and it made him sound grumpy. He muttered, 'Rather a crazy man, but he did try to help.'

Clara was watching her father. He said, *'Crazy?'* – and she could tell by the way the smile had suddenly gone from his eyes, by his alert and listening face, that this wasn't a light word to him. Perhaps, whatever her mother had said, he would have guessed about David. Guessed there was *something* wrong, anyway. But who was going to tell him? Not Grandpa. Noel had said all he was going to. And Liz, like Bosie, had put it behind her. She was concentrating on her lemon pie.

'Up to me,' Clara thought. She looked at her family, all safely together at last. A pity to spoil this happy party! She thought how much David would have liked to be here, and how very glad she felt that he wasn't. If that was sad, she could do nothing about it. Nor could her mother and father. But if she stayed silent, they would never know what had happened. They would be kept in the dark! 'Well,' she thought, 'serve them right! They've kept us in the dark before now.' For what they would say was 'good reason'.

She had good reason, too. It would upset her parents to

know they had been so frightened. In danger. And it would hurt Grandpa terribly. He would hate them to know that he hadn't been master of the house, always.

She said, 'David was tiresome, Dad. Noel says "crazy". He only means he was a bit potty, sometimes. But Grandpa knew how to manage him. In Rome you do what the Romans do, and Grandpa is the Chief Roman.'